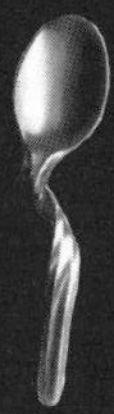

cake & prostheses

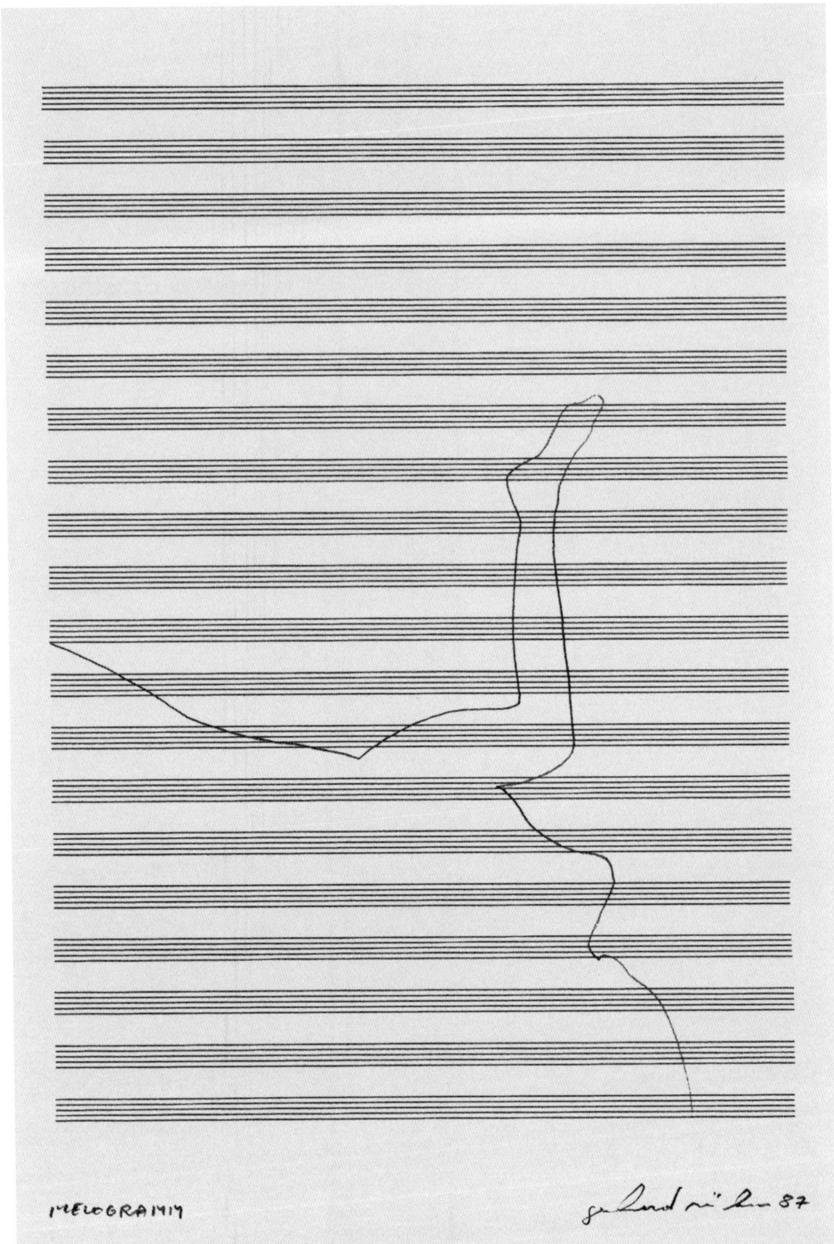
MELOGRAMM
87

GERHARD RÜHM

CAKE & PROSTHESES

mini dramas and short prose

translated from the german by

ALEXANDER BOOTH

TWISTED SPOON PRESS
PRAGUE
2024

ISBN: 978-80-88628-02-6
ISBN: 978-80-88628-33-0 (e-book)

This publication was supported by a grant from the Federal Ministry of Arts, Culture, Civil Service and Sport of the Republic of Austria.

Federal Ministry
Republic of Austria
Arts, Culture,
Civil Service and Sport

CONTENTS

THREE PEOPLE SEEKING A GOOD MOOD
mini dramas

HERO READS GRILLPARZER / LEANDER LEARNS TO SWIM
a classic love story

CAKE AND PROSTHESES
two dozen short prose texts

three people seeking a good mood

mini dramas

aphoristic scenes

tablesonatina

props :
a little table with a metal plate, matchbox, sparkler, bottle of piccolo sekt, slender sekt glass; microphone(s) to amplify the sound.

1st movement

the bottle of sekt is opened. the glass is slowly filled, the bottle put back in place.

2nd movement

two matches are removed from the matchbox. one is bent in the middle, the other is used to light the sparkler.

3rd movement

before the sparkler goes out, it is dipped into the sekt glass. the sekt glass is knocked over and breaks. the sonatina ends when no more drops fall onto the ground and it is quiet.

each movement is announced.

teleclavier

ten thin strips of transparent cellulose tape are attached to ten white keys of a piano — from middle c upwards : c, e, g. h, d, f, a c, e, g. the other ends are attached to the fingers of the "player," who is sitting on a piano stool at a distance from the keyboard and pressing down the aforementioned keys by moving the strips at regular intervals. the connection will not last long, the thin strips of tape will gradually loosen due to the repeated pressure and float to the ground. once the final connecting strip has torn, the piece is over. for a little while you will still be able to hear the final note.

piano-strip-music

two pianos (without lids) with their keyboards parallel to each other. between them, at the level of the depressed keys, a narrow connecting board (with supports from below), which, together with the keyboards, offers enough space for a reclining actress. before the piece begins, with the stage or podium in total darkness, the actress lies motionless on the two keyboards with her feet stretched out toward the public. she is wearing evening clothes, possibly a coat, scarf and hat as well. in the middle, in front of the two pianos, a piano stool.

once the podium has been illuminated the pianist, who has only an auxiliary function in this piece, stands in front of the stool, like a conductor with back to the audience. following the pianist's hand signal the actress, still on the keys, begins to disrobe, which is what creates the piece. the pianist takes each piece of clothing and places it on the stool. once the actress is nude, she lies down again and remains motionless in the resting position while the pianist depresses and fixes the right pedal of both pianos.

with overlapping reverberations, the action then proceeds backwards. the pianist hands the actress her clothing piece by piece. once she is fully clothed, she returns to her starting position. as soon as the reverberations have faded, the stage is darkened.

the resulting piano piece is recorded throughout the action and then played back through loudspeakers to be perceived purely as music.

momentary darknesses

1

i attempt to delay the organic blinking of my eyelids for as long as possible. this is filmed for a period of time in close-up.

2

the film is shown. every time my eyelids close briefly i scream. this is recorded by audio.

3

i listen to the recording — with closed eyes that, every time i hear a scream, i jerk open fearfully.

transference

lying on a piece of white cardboard, i outline my body in black pen. then the drawing is attached to a wall and lashed with a five-tailed whip, each tail with a pencil affixed at its tips, until the pencils become blunt.

communication

a female hand masturbating a penis.
the moment the man comes he moans : “yessssss.”

nature study

curtain rises.
defloration.
curtain falls.

a piece for two

curtain rises.
one clothed and one nude person come onstage from opposite sides and pass each other by — the clothed one resolvedly, the nude one hesitantly — without any sign of acknowledgment.
before either one leaves the stage, the nude person turns to the clothed person for a moment, the clothed person to the nude for somewhat longer.
curtain falls.

a comedy

a number of people sitting onstage.
as if noticing something strange, one person looks a little more closely at another, then points and laughs. then the person laughed at points at a third and laughs in turn (when the next person is pointed at, the previous one falls silent). the previous person laughed at now points at another and laughs, etc., until each person has pointed and laughed at everyone else.
a moment of awkward silence.
then everyone laughs.
curtain falls.

a drama in five acts

curtain rises.
on the darkened stage five people standing next to one another. each of them holding a burning candle in their hand.
after a little while, the second person (from the left) blows the first person's candle out. exit first person.
now the third person blows the second person's candle out. exit second person.
the fourth person blows the third person's candle out. exit third person.
the fifth person blows the fourth person's candle out. exit fourth person.
the fifth person looks around for a little while, at a loss. then blows their own candle out. total darkness.
curtain falls.

flower piece

curtain rises.
in the middle of the stage a little side table. on it a vase filled with water in which there is a bouquet of flowers. for a good while nothing happens.
suddenly (from the backdrop) the vase is shot.
curtain falls.

a family drama

a mannequin lying on a wooden block, in front of it a basket. a man's naked arm (the rest of the body is hidden by a black curtain) lops off the mannequin's head with a hatchet. as soon as it falls into the basket, a brief "goal!" rings out from a loudspeaker (an original recording from a soccer match).
curtain falls.

presence

light :
2.9 seconds!
dark.

timing

curtain rises.
on a long table twenty-four alarm clocks displaying the current time. behind them just as many people holding raised hammers. as soon as the alarm clocks ring, they strike and then listen to the ensuing quiet.
curtain falls.

fall study

curtain rises.
a man standing on a stool. in each of his outstretched hands an unopened bottle of beer. on the ground beneath his one hand a wooden board, beneath his other a board of stone. first he lets a bottle of beer fall on the wood, then the other onto the stone. once the bang has faded, two pieces of blotting paper fall out of his hands. once they've reached the ground, he sits down on the stool and assumes a thinking position.
curtain falls.

money piece

against the sides and back of the stage wide, head-high wardrobes with narrow drawers from bottom to top, not unlike coin cabinets.
as soon as all the members of the audience have taken their seats, a voice comes over the loudspeaker :
"in one of these drawers there is a real one-thousand euro bill. get on up here and try to find it — finders, keepers."

memory piece

while sitting in the open compartment of a high-speed train halfway between two stops stand up on your seat and say, quietly but assuredly, "now" and then sit back down. when you reach the next stop, change trains and repeat the action at the same point while traveling in the other direction with the word "once."

the wardrobe

curtain rises.
in the middle of the stage, floodlit, a massive, two-door wardrobe.
— — —
at the first sounds of impatience from the audience the doors fly open, and a massive pile of coal (which fills up the entire wardrobe) crashes onto the floor of the stage.
curtain falls.

practiced biblical saying

catechist : love thy neighbor as thyself.
exegete : i hate myself! (gives the former a hard hook to the chin that crumples him to the floor).

a relationship drama

woman with cigarette to her staggering husband :
  "alcohol you the devil!"
man, glassy-eyed, haltingly :
  "cig-a-rette me!"
a pungent swath of grey nicotine envelops them. a suffocating, chronic cough ends the discussion.

misguided seduction

a historical play

under an artificial tree with several leaves and a single, conspicuously attached apple stand adam and eve. both nude, of course, but with their genitals covered by fig leaves which are held in place around their buttocks by rubber bands. a paper snake is curled around the trunk. at a distance a rather large, cardboard tyrannosaurus rex.

after a while of stillness an angel pulls a wind machine onstage and begins to steadily increase its settings. just as eve — jerkily, like a mannequin — reaches up to pluck the apple, it falls to the ground, torn loose by a stronger gust of wind, and bursts with a heavy thunderclap. fallen fruit that has become all too soft.

after that, the angel hurries off with the wind machine.

after a brief scare, adam emits a disappointed sigh :

"now it's : they stuck around!"

eve, foolishly naïve, in a blasé tone :

". . . — in paradise . . ."

they stand around a little longer, indecisively. then the curtain falls.

ideal couple

preceded by a few things.
she : i've got time . . .
he : i've got space . . .
the two embrace and kiss.

making the rounds

fräulein kleinlein (the name is irrelevant) is sitting on one side of the couch. her partner on the other.
after some time, the clock strikes eleven. fräulein kleinlein stands up and leaves through the door to the left of the dimly lit room.
five minutes later there is a knock on one of the glass windows. fräulein kleinlein's partner stands up, goes to the middle of the outer wall and pulls back the curtain. behind the now visible window fräulein kleinlein's head — she's the one who knocked. her partner opens the window and goes back to their place on the couch. as if from out of the depths fräulein kleinlein climbs over the windowsill into the room and, as is her wont, takes her place back on the couch.
after some time — not a word is spoken — the clock strikes twelve. fräulein kleinlein's partner gets up, goes to the open window, climbs up onto the sill, and jumps. we hear his piercing, sustained yell and steep plummet into the reverberant lightwell. following the muffled impact, five minutes of quiet.
then there is a claw-like scratching at the door, which grows ever more insistent. fräulein kleinlein gets up, as always, wholly impassively, to open it. a menacing looking dog trots through the room to the couch, jumps up, and sits down in the corner where fräulein kleinlein's partner once sat.

progress

from the left, a female clucking (like a hen) and at the same time, from the right, a male crowing (like a rooster). when they meet in the center of the stage, both fall onto all fours and continue, the one meowing (like a cat) and the other barking (like a dog), on their separate ways until they disappear in opposite directions. immediately thereafter, parting the curtain that closes to the back, they reappear together as woman and man with the words :

"yeah?"
"no!"
"no?"
"yeah!"

they walk straight toward the audience. just before they reach the edge of the stage, the curtain falls.

the open door

the curtain rises on an empty stage. in the middle of the back wall an open door giving onto darkness. across from it, almost by the forestage, a person in evening clothes sitting with their back to the audience — apparently staring spellbound into the dark . . .
after around five to ten minutes, they stand up and walk silently in slow motion toward the door. once there, they abruptly slam it : the technically amplified boom makes the audience seats tremble. all the lights go out. the curtain falls.

an elementary duel

dressed in a red leotard, a pack of cigarettes and a box of matches in hand, the firebug is standing across from the waterman who's dressed in a blue leotard and holding a garden hose. their tête-à-tête takes place on a thatched roof (extending across the whole stage).

finger to chest the firebug turns toward the audience :

> i'm the eager
> trouble driver,
> spark spitter
> flame slinger,
> stripping countries clean
> leaving dwellings lean,
> a grown griper
> no shitty piker!

the waterman, pointing confidently at himself :

> as a wet water-sprayer
> i was, am, and will be
> a snappy grasper
> and insightful minder,
> a badass fire-dismisser
> a brilliant water-pisser —
> (turning toward the firebug)
> you dead-end nipper!

firebug :

> pretty slick, but me i'm slicker,
> over rooftops and ruins
> this sick flamethrower flickers.
> i burn for risk!

things'll get redder, not bluer,
just like last year so in this!
(to the audience)
it ain't for free, it's steep —
but no tax charged, at least.
no barn, no harm,
always new sheep in the shire,
so i commend myself for hire,
on your command a fire!

the firebug ostentatiously lights a cigarette then deliberately tosses the still burning match into the straw, which promptly catches fire. the waterman quickly reacts by turning on the hose and extinguishing it. then the firebug drops his burning cigarette. once again, the waterman puts it out. the firebug hurriedly lights a new cigarette and, as before, tosses the match to the ground. the waterman continues to spray, even the next cigarette. burning matches and cigarettes follow one another now in quick succession, and the waterman is constantly busy putting out flames. gradually, the stage begins to drip and all the water pouring out of the hose runs down into the auditorium. the firebug's chances of finding dry spots for his fiery obsession begin to dwindle. eventually, his last cigarette is brutally sprayed out of his face. sobbing loudly, he flees the stage.

our waterman presents himself as the rightful winner — albeit at the expense of the audience in the front rows.

slide show for woman man child
or
the ten commandments

slide : a halved blood orange as seen from the front of its sliced planes
boy :
    and if i lend an ear
    will there be something for me to hear?
mother :
    you know better than to ask,
    i'm not allowed to tell you that.

slide : a sliced piece of blood sausage
boy :
    and if it bursts,
    tell me, will you die of thirst?
father :
    you know better than to ask,
    i've got no response to that.

slide : bloodhound, a pitbull's slobbering mouth toward the viewer
boy :
    what a nasty mouth!
    what is it that makes him growl?
mother :
    you know better than to ask,
    i'm not allowed to tell you that.

slide : a bloody leech on a human body (image from an old medical reference book)
boy :
    is what i'm seeing a flail
    or is it something with a tail?

father :

you know better than to ask,
i've got no response to that.

slide : bloodstream (schematic medical image)
boy :

and what's all this i'm seeing here?
something we must accept with cheer?

mother :

you know better than to ask,
i'm not allowed to tell you that.

slide : martyr (naïve depiction of a blood-spattered figure from a catholic devotional)
boy :

is the one there nursing
going to go on and curtsy?

father :

you know better than to ask,
i've got no response to that.

slide : a bloody sanitary napkin
boy :

is that the resin-smeared rind
of a big old lime?

mother :

you know better than to ask,
i'm not allowed to tell you that.

slide : vampire, sucking blood from a woman's neck (film still)
boy :

and what's all this?
is it some kind of kiss?

father :

you know better than to ask,
i've got no response to that.

slide : donator of blood with the requisite device on their arm

boy :

do people in the british lands
also wear those kinds of bands?

mother :

you know better than to ask,
i'm not allowed to tell you that.

slide : a nude man bound to a cross, doused in blood (color photo of a nitsch action)

boy :

what's he up to, dad?
is it something bad?

father :

come on, as if you had to ask!
i've got nothing at all to say about that!

boy, defiant :

fine, if you don't want to play
i'll just see what uncle hermann has to say!

he leaves the stage, offended.

perplexed, the mother and father look at each other and shrug.

postlude

(this can also be read by an external party)

the boy comes back onstage with his sister in tow — both of them nude — to commit incest.

at the same time, their mother and father, now similarly nude, take a bath full of blood.

no curtain, the shocking scene of magnificent hemorrhage is simply covered up.

un

a mi-gration song for two
across the boards that represent the world

plot

after a short silence, the piano is played (see stave below). immediately following the last note, the stage lights are turned on. on the stage or podium (an arena stage is also conceivable as a performance location), a large circle has been drawn, at the outer points of which two nude people (or people dressed in full-body leotards) are standing : on the left — facing the audience — the woman, on the right — back to the audience — the man. both immediately begin to move in a circular, counterclockwise direction. after the first circle, once they've returned to the starting point, she utters the syllable "un" on treble c, and after the second circle, he utters the syllable "un" on tenor c. in a total of sixteen rounds, each person says "un" eight times in turn — she one tone lower on the diatonic scale, he one tone higher, so that eventually both (he after her) reach the same tone, middle c. then a *fortissimo* cluster is heard on the piano (with the pedal depressed, all the white keys, from tenor to treble c, are struck simultaneously). both now turn inward and walk slowly toward each other. once face to face, they say "at last" and embrace. after the sound of the chord has faded, a little while longer and darkness.
the model-like piece is not to be performed sententiously or even parodically, but with the concentration and artificial clarity of "concrete poetry."

ff

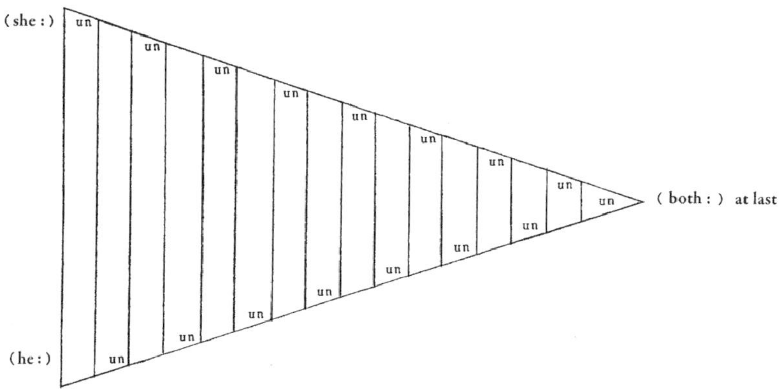
(she :)
un
un
un
un
un
un
un
un
un
(both :) at last
(he :)
un
un
un
un
un
un
un
un
un

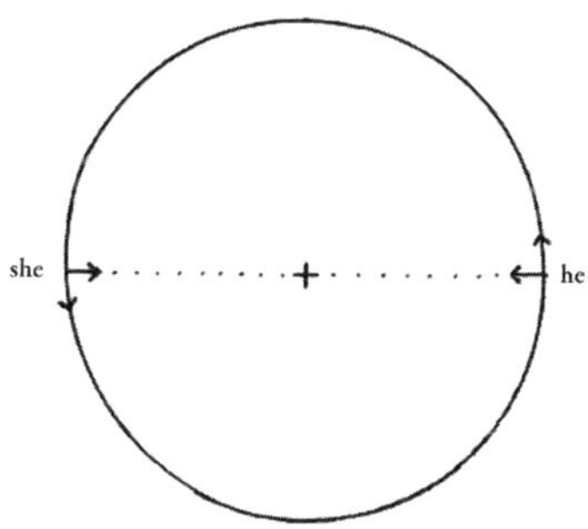
she
he

the note of notes

scene for a piano player and a woman reading the paper

onstage a piano and stool as well as a freestanding chair, upon which there is a copy of (today's) paper.

from memory a piano player plays the notes reproduced below, as if attempting to find a forgotten sequence. once he reaches "f sharp," he stops, lets it reverberate and strikes it again and again — with occasional, though not too long, pauses. he listens intently to every note.
soon a woman appears from the left, as if she just wanted to cross the room. arriving at the stool, she pauses, notices the paper, grabs it and begins to leaf through it. lingering on a particular piece of news, she slowly sits down. for a while nothing but the note, repeated with a differentiated, but always unobtrusive tone.
eventually, with a slightly ironic undertone, the woman says to the piano player :

"there are piano players who know how to play other notes, too."

without any hint of irritation he replies :

"that's because they're still looking for the right one."

she then begins to read out loud random headlines and summaries from the paper. when she reaches the last page, she tears the paper vertically in half, crumples each sheet and forms balls that she teasingly throws in the piano player's direction. once her ammunition is spent, she stands up and leaves the room, slowly taking her time.
he continues to play a while longer . . .

alternative ending

the woman remains seated and begins to listen ever more devoutly to the sounds while the room gradually fades into darkness. the sound continues until the last spectator has left their seat.

three people seeking a good mood

a rectangular table. a lady sits in the middle, to her left and right a gentleman (in profile). after a while of embarrassed silence

the man on the left :
the married couple had booked a two-week cruise.
in the morning she asks : "what day is it today, karlheinz?"
"monday."
"then that there is genoa."

the woman (after brief reflection) :
knepke comes home a little earlier than usual and catches his wife in bed with the super.
he : "what's going on here?"
she : "your watch is running a little quick."

the man on the right (almost on top of her) :
"what time is it?"
"in twelve minutes it'll be nine-thirty."
"i don't want to know what time it'll be in twelve minutes but what time it is now."

the man on the left (immediately) :
the last of summer's balmy nights in the city park.
birgit whispers to her friend : "do you hear the crickets chirping?"
"crickets?" he chuckles, "those are zippers."

the woman :
a very pregnant woman walks into the butcher shop : "i'd like some blood sausage."
the saleswoman opines : "your husband will be surprised."

the man on the right :
"do you know french?"
"yes."
"but that's english."
"oh, i know that, too?"

the man on the left :
the absent-minded professor to a colleague : "my daughter wrote me that she's had a baby. but not whether it's a boy or a girl. i have no idea whether i'm a grandpa or a grandma."

the woman :
frau weber is reading the horoscope. she reproachfully says to her husband : "why didn't you come into the world two days earlier? you would've been witty and charming."

the man on the right :
"the tailor's outside with the bill. he doesn't intend to leave until he's got his money," the servant reports.
"fine, johann," the count replies, "then make up the guest room for him, please."

the man on the left :
manfred puts his boots out in front of his hotel-room door to be cleaned. the next morning he finds one brown and one black boot. angered, he approaches the porter.
"what a coincidence," the latter replies, "earlier this morning someone else complained about the exact same thing."

the woman :
the müller's dog is all by himself at home. the phone rings. he picks up and says : "woof!"
the caller is confused : "excuse me?"

the dog replies : " 'w' as in 'wilhelm', double 'o' as in 'oscar', 'f' as in 'fritz.' "

the man on the right :
press conference.
a professor reports : "we've managed the impossible : we've crossed a woodpecker with a pigeon."
"and?" a journalist asks.
the professor : "well, now we've finally got a carrier pigeon that knocks before delivering the mail."

the man on the left :
"imagine : yesterday i'm at the races, next to the track, i bend over to tie a shoelace. a jockey comes over and saddles me."
"and?"
"i came in second."

the woman :
frau moser is letting her maidservant go : "i am very sorry, but, among other things, we have gotten a vacuum cleaner that will replace you."
the maidservant replies : "that will be quite an adjustment for your husband."

the man on the right :
peter and paul go on a cruise together. in the evenings, peter puts on a woman's nightgown.
"why do you do that?" paul wonders.
"well, if the ship goes down, women and children get rescued first."

the man on the left :
a young man approaches a young woman in a bar : "miss, i'm compiling a phone book. may i ask you for your name and address, please?"

the woman :

the head secretary is in the hospital and receives a visit from her colleague. worried, she asks "everything going ok at the office?"
"not to worry. we've divvied up your workload : claudia is in charge of the coffee, birgit is working on your sweater, stephanie is doing the crossword, and i'm sleeping with the boss."

the man on the right :

the client is upset : "i bought a stool here yesterday and it's already broken!"
the salesperson thinks for a moment : "did someone sit on it perchance?"

the man on the left :

"certain abilities," the professor says to his students, "are inherited. if you are unable to have children, for example, it could be that your parents' marriage remained childless, too."

the woman :

a woman on a luxury cruise is keeping a diary. she writes :
august 4 : walked along the deck.
august 5 : met the captain. a fetching man.
august 6 : the captain gave me a lot of compliments.
august 7 : the captain invited me to dinner.
august 8 : the captain has become pushy.
august 9 : the captain is threatening to capsize the ship if i don't sleep with him.
august 10 : today i saved 824 lives.

the man on the right :

heinrich meets up with an old buddy : "where did you spend your summer holidays this year?"
"italy."
"how interesting. does that country really look like a boot?"

the man on the left :
two police officers out on patrol pass by a house where one of them lives. the one points upstairs and says : "i live up there. the person on the balcony is my wife, and the man next to her — that's me."

the woman :
frau kunze goes to the electrician and complains : "i've been asking you to repair my doorbell for weeks!"
"i've already been by four times — but no one comes to open up."

the man on the right :
frau schulze goes to the greengrocer in a fluster : "yesterday my husband was supposed to pick up a package of spinach and hasn't been back since."
the saleswoman : "go ahead and take a can of peas."

the man on the left :
the doctor to their overweight patient : "you can lose up to thirty kilos by walking five kilometers a day."
three-hundred days later they receive a frantic phone call : "that thing about the weight worked, but now I've got a different problem."
"what now?"
"i'm one-thousand-five-hundred kilometers away from home!"

the woman :
two older women are sitting by a boxing ring. one of the boxers falls to the mat. the referee starts to count.
one of the two older women calls out : "he's not getting up! i know him from the tram."

the man on the right :
a man goes to the psychiatrist : "herr doctor, i'm psychic. it's making me crazy."

"how long have you had this problem?"
"since the day after tomorrow."

the man on the left :
at the school party johannes asks his teacher to dance.
"i will not dance with a child," she says, turning him away.
johannes apologizes : "i'm sorry, i didn't realize you were expecting.'

the woman :
"is it nice to be married to an archeologist?"
"oh, is it! the older i get, the more interested he grows."

the man on the right :
irate phone call to the weather service : "could you finally make a forecast that actually comes true?!"
"gladly. toward evening, increasing darkness is to be expected."

the man on the left :
the married couple had booked a two-week cruise.
in the morning she asks : "what day is today, karlheinz?"
"monday."
"then that there is . . ."

the woman :
we've already heard this one!

the man on the left :
you sure?

the man on the right :
very sure.

the man on the left :
then i can go.
he stands up and exits stage left.

the woman (calls after him) :
but i know another one!

the woman and the man on the right look at each other, baffled.
after a brief moment of silence

the woman says :
knepke comes home a little earlier than usual and catches his wife in bed with the super.
he : "what's going on here?"
she : "your watch is running a little quick."

the man on the right :
we already had that one, too.

the woman stands up silently and, somewhat hurt, exits stage left.

the man on the right pensively watches her go and then repeats his last joke to himself (in a somewhat subdued tone). with every repetition, it grows a bit darker until the darkness is complete.

the man on the right :
phone call to the weather service : "could you finally make a forecast that actually comes true?!"
"gladly. toward evening, increasing darkness is to be expected."
—
phone call to the weather service : "could you finally make a forecast that actually comes true?!"
"gladly. toward evening, increasing darkness is to be expected."

—

phone call to the weather service : "could you finally make a forecast that actually comes true?!"
"gladly. toward evening, increasing darkness is to be expected."

—

phone call to the weather service : "could you finally make a forecast that actually comes true?!"
"gladly. toward evening, increasing darkness is to be expected."

—

"toward evening, increasing darkness is to be expected."

—

"increasing darkness is to be expected."

—

"increasing darkness."

—

"darkness."

coffee klatch

playlet for two young women

a room with a window in the back wall. two chairs and a table with a white tablecloth. on it stand a narrow boot-shaped vase containing a pretty paper flower, a coffee pot, two full coffee cups with small spoons, a sugar bowl with plenty of sugar, two cake plates, each with a slice of jam cake. in addition, a not unsizable ashtray and a matchbox. on the somewhat slanted right-hand wall hangs an easily recognizable picture (color photo) of a family — mother, father, child — at the table.
on the two chairs dressed in comfortable, everyday casual wear sit ilse (the hostess) and ulla, who is just taking out a cigarette. ilse obligingly lights a match, but ulla crushes the unsmoked cigarette in the ashtray, into which ilse then puts the burning match.

ilse
the nimble weasel dashes across the tiles and over the table into the middle of the winterly meadow where, in crevices, circa seven, in the meanwhile maybe seventy widows are sitting and freezing their arms full of shrill bells, ham, and lilies.

ulla
at the north pole, it is currently dark for 24 hours a day — and much too mild. at the time of the last measurement, it was two to four degrees celsius — above-freezing, mind you. the temperatures at the northernmost point of the earth at this time of year are minus 30 to 40 degrees celsius. researchers from the american weather service NOAA think it's possible that the deviation from normal values could even reach up to 50 degrees in the next few days. the earth's system is responding to small changes in carbon dioxide levels more radically than previous climate models predicted.

ulla takes out another cigarette. ilse lights a match, and when ulla again carelessly crushes the unsmoked cigarette ilse puts the burning match into the ashtray.

ilse
once again the wind-whipped treetops sway while to the left in spite of the storm a line of wonky deer joneses for food.

ulla
chelsea fires coach josé mourinho "by mutual agreement," as it was so well put yesterday. after 16 matches, chelsea is in sixteenth place with only 15 points and four wins. the eccentric mourinho had been in charge of the blues for the second time since june 2013. the portuguese coach's contract was to run until 2019. a severance package of 50 million euros is being discussed!

ulla takes out another cigarette. ilse lights a match, and when ulla again carelessly crushes the cigarette ilse puts the burning match into the ashtray.

ilse
from the ship a viennese woman in go-go boots giggles and tosses her lipstick to the similarly tittering fish, who, visibly confused, begin to play with it.

ulla
great britain plays out its latest military triumph in the southern afghan province of helmand. the internationally feared SAS are always deployed when the situation is desperate. and the situation is desperate : the radical islamic taliban have largely taken control of the strategically important city of sangin, are attacking the U.S. base at bagram, and firing rockets at kabul.

ulla takes out a cigarette. ilse lights a match, and when ulla again carelessly crushes the cigarette ilse puts the burning match into the ashtray.

ilse

with a grin and tiny umbrella between his fingers her darling mistakenly steps into a fresh pile of shit; back there, in the dark, four sensational singers from mississippi are singing intimate songs of light while waving their wings.

ulla

the thuringian village of drogen has to come up with a new town sign. once again, thieves have "professionally" removed the former one at the entrance to the village. officials are investigating the case as one of grand larceny. in the past, the signs had already been in demand due to the town's curious name.

ulla takes out a cigarette. ilse lights a match, and when ulla carelessly crushes the cigarette ilse puts the burning match into the ashtray.

ilse

with his brush a made-up pianist intimately taps the currants until they bloom a cute violin in the mirror.

ulla

burning cities, fleeing civilians, roaring tanks : war is raging in eastern turkey. the government is using brutal force against kurdish separatists. more than 100 people have died in the last few days. a few months ago, everything was still going well : the government was negotiating with the kurds for a peaceful future. the pro-kurdish left-wing peoples' democratic party's landslide victory, however, was humiliating for president recep tayyip erdogan. since then, the turkish air force has been bombing kurdish militias in syria. and the army has attacked turkish cities such as silvan, cizre and silopi as well as the kurdish metropolis of diyarbakir. a curfew has been in place for weeks. snipers are firing on civilians, entire city districts have been shelled and destroyed by heavy artillery. the magnificent old city of diyarbakir, just recently declared a world heritage site, is now a war zone. the horrified human rights activist abdusselam inceören is unequivocal : "they show no consideration for women, children or the old. the attacks are aimed at the kurdish people." in germany, criticism is coming from the opposition. green party leader cem özdemir speaks of a "war against turkey's own population. they can arrest whomever they want, torture whomever they want, kill whomever they want."

ulla takes out a cigarette. ilse lights a match. when ulla carelessly crushes the cigarette, ilse puts the burning match into the ashtray.

ilse
cunningly, the dirndl-clad crook escapes with a package of pillows from the sticky elevator into the balmy sky.

ulla
not even mayor of the mexican city of temixco for 24 hours and 33-year-old gisela mota was already dead. several gunmen broke into the house of the local politician and shot her. mota had previously declared war on organized crime.

ulla takes out a cigarette. ilse lights a match. while ulla crushes the cigarette in the ashtray, ilse sets fire to the paper flower in the vase.

ulla
following the paris attacks, the country cannot rest. belgian police have arrested ten terror suspects. eleven houses have been searched in the northeast of the country, the belgian public prosecutor's office announced in brussels on thursday. the prosecutor's office did not

initially provide any information on the identities of those arrested nor their backgrounds. meanwhile, belgium's radio station RTBF reported that the suspected paris bomber narrowly escaped the belgian police days after the terrorist attacks. he is said to have hidden behind a piece of furniture.

ilse smears the jam-filled side of her piece of cake against the picture on the wall and lets the rest fall to the floor.

ulla
the second most populous state in the U.S., texas, now permits the open carry of firearms. with a new law that went into effect on january 1, guns may now be openly carried in holsters, on belts or around one's shoulder when working, shopping or eating out in a restaurant.

ilse empties the entire sugar bowl into ulla's coffee cup so that the coffee spills onto the tablecloth.

ulla
poland's most famous civil rights activist and former president lech wałęsa has sharply criticized the actions of the new right-wing government, even warning of a civil war. the planned reforms must be carried out "openly and democratically" and not, as before, in a "brutal way." wałęsa was referring to the planned reform of the constitutional court. germany's government is also shocked and appalled by the new radical right-wing course poland is taking. a cabinet member told the weekly news magazine *der spiegel* : "what is happening in warsaw at the moment confirms our worst fears." the attempt to exert influence on the judiciary and the press is very similar to hungary's right-wing populist prime minister viktor orbán.

ilse smashes the vase in two.

ulla
rokstan was 17 when she was abducted and raped by three soldiers in syria. but in her family, which had been living in germany for a number of years, instead of comfort and care all she received every day were beatings and savage insults. she was "unclean, tainted." so the young woman fled — and fell in love. then her own mother ordered her murder. two months ago, rokstan's body was found in a gazebo in dessau — she had been stabbed to death. per the investigation, in dessau she was to be subjected to a forced marriage. the fact that the fiancé did not show up was presumably the kurdish woman's death sentence. her father has since gone into hiding.

ilse takes a handsaw from the table drawer and saws off a chair leg.

ulla
according to the syrian observatory for human rights, for more than 170 days madaya, northwest of the capital damascus, has been held by regime troops and the lebanese shiite militia, hezbollah. 40,000 people — about half of them civilians — are currently living in the city, which is under heavy bombardment due to the presence of rebels. according to media reports, minefields and a strict surveillance system are preventing food from being imported and the inhabitants from fleeing. thousands of syrians are threatened with starvation. a doctor from madaya told the german press agency that residents in the city were eating grass to satisfy their hunger. in addition, just a few days ago, they had begun to slaughter cats and dogs.

ilse pulls ulla up from her chair, slits her clothes from top to bottom and, sitting back down, pulls her onto her lap.

ulla
on new year's eve more than one thousand north-african and arabic-looking men had gathered in front of cologne's main train station. while

bottles and firecrackers flew indiscriminately into the crowd from the cathedral steps, women were surrounded by small groups of drunk, disinhibited men, sexually harassed, insulted and robbed. shortly after midnight, the first victims reported to the understaffed and hopelessly overwhelmed police. crying and shocked, the women described how they had been sexually assaulted. a twenty-year-old from stuttgart had had her panties torn off and her lower body touched in an indecent manner. whenever the perpetrators were pointed out, the victims and witnesses were threatened on the spot or stalked afterward. scenes never before seen in germany. well over a hundred women have filed complaints with the police in the last few days. in two cases, rape is being investigated. the sexual assaults are causing general consternation.

ilse hurls the full ashtray out of the (closed) window. the pane shatters. from outside, as if from a neighboring apartment, comes the sound of the chanson "feeling blue" (see below). tenderly nestled together, both women listen to the sounds. at the end, curtain (if no curtain is available, dark).

(feeling blue)

a stoat
a loach
a lynx
and a fox
just sitting there
with a mute stare
because to my dismay
i'm such awful company today

the weather is shite
nothing at all is right
like i'm on standby

and i don't know why
i'm in a frosty mood
been silent for days
but there's something to say
and i whisper
whisper to my dismay
that i'm such a bad companion today
the stoat
and the loach
the lynx
and the fox
just sitting there
nodding a lidless stare

stimmungstief [feeling blue]

fros-tig die lau-ne nach län - ge - rem schwei-gen muss man sich zei-gen und ich
rau - ne rau - ne mit trü - bem sinn dass ich ein schlech-ter ge - sell - schaf - ter bin
der dachs und der lachs der luchs
und der fuchs hok - ken he - rum und nik - ken nur stumm
8va
8vb
pp

lunar theater

preface

the lunar pieces are intended for four astronaut performers. they are to be broadcast live by terrestrial television stations in various time slots.

capitulation piece

the astronauts aboard the "mare crisium" have hoisted a white flag and until further notice have assumed the "hands up!" position.

communion

the astronauts fan out in all four directions to find god within the moon's stillness.
after a considerable amount of time
and a fruitless search they meet up again at their point of departure.

ritual measurement of the earth

between two fingers the commander measures the diameter of the earth as soon as it touches the horizon. then looks for a small stone of the same size. once found, he shows it to the others and tells them to follow his example. having done so, they all stand next to one another and, looking at the setting earth, raise their hands with the small stone between thumb and forefinger. as soon as the earth has disappeared, they throw their small stones after it.

rebus

the astronauts stick twenty-two sticks into the ground equidistant so that there is a space between the third and fifth sticks, three spaces between the twelfth and sixteenth sticks. then everyone stands behind an empty space while holding an artificial flower.

first the astronaut in position thirteen places a poppy flower in the sand and takes a step back;

then the astronaut in position fifteen places an orchid and takes two steps back;

their neighbor in position fourteen a carnation, takes three steps back;

lastly, the astronaut in position four a dahlia, and takes four steps back.

after a minute of silence with a view of the flowers they all leave the playing field.

dialogue for the clamoring citizens of earth

delivered very calmly and evenly.

astronaut 1 :

found
ground

astronaut 2 :

knows
names

astronaut 3 :

thin
rim

astronaut 4 :

are
blind

astronaut 1 :

hand
commands

astronaut 2 :

grit
kitsch

astronaut 3 :

burns
turns

astronaut 4 :

raw
maw

astronaut 1 :

balmy
breeze

astronaut 2 :

balled
bundle

astronaut 3 :

throne
boon

astronaut 4 :

home
moon.

throughout the exchange only the empty lunar landscape is visible.

a children's piece

the "mare humorum" with a view of the disastrous "doppelmayr" wall.

the 1st astronaut :

dotty, dotty (makes two dots next to each other in the lunar dust),

the 2nd astronaut :

dashy (beneath the two dots, in the middle, draws a vertical dash),

the 3rd astronaut :

dashy (beneath the vertical dash draws a horizontal one),

the 4th astronaut :

(draws a circle around them all) moonfacey?

attempt at a folk dance

the astronauts aboard the "mare tranquillitatis" dress a mannequin that they've brought along in a bavarian-style dirndl. to the best of their ability they attempt to dance a schuhplattler around it to show that, despite their bulky space suits, on the moon they can jump higher than those folks down in bavaria can.

attempt at a performance of "hamlet" on the moon

an astronaut with a broom is sweeping moon dust and stones from the surface of a human-sized grave into a pile.
another looks on thoughtfully.
the third brings all the national flags of the earth in toy format out from the lunar lander and dumps them on the swept rectangle.
while the first covers the flags with the piled-up garbage
the fourth astronaut appears as hamlet (represented by a black flag with light gray lettering spelling out "hamlet") and stretched as far as possible recites :

> "to be — — — or — — — not to be — — — here — — — that — — — is — — — the question — — —."

situational pantomime

shortly before the pitch-black lunar night descends – it will last the equivalent of fourteen earth days – the astronauts bid farewell to the daylight with a carefully rehearsed, elegiacal pantomime whose various climaxes, however, demonstrate new dance possibilities thanks to the sixfold gravity reduction.

sports piece

the four astronauts stand in a row. at a sign, each of them jumps as far as they can (a particular joy on the moon).
whoever wins will be able to assume command of a further moon flight, the next two runners-up are eliminated,
the last one has to stay behind on the moon and try to reach the "bayer" crater – the final destination. to make the loneliness more bearable, an employee of the control center will help by reading via satellite the seventh chapter of the novel *the rocket to the moon* by thea von harbou – and even more of it for as long as the oxygen in the tank on the astronaut's back lasts.

puppet plays

cutlery play

for table theater

onstage a simple wooden table (its drawer facing the audience) just big enough for a table setting. a soup plate with steaming soup (underneath a dinner plate?), next to it, on the right, a knife and spoon, on the left, a fork and napkin, in front, a teaspoon.

knife : male voice
fork : female voice
spoon : male voice
teaspoon : child's voice
soup : female voice
table : male voice (sound source beneath the tabletop)

as opposed to the table's prose the verses are recited in a jaunty singsongy tone.
the objects can be held by black-gloved hands (arms in black leotard) or from above by (nylon) cords.

the piece takes place during a cutlery trade fair in gablitz and then continues via the town of haslach and its pointy spoons through the gailtal valley on to nassfeld.

the table :

i, table, am of natural origin. according to legend once upon a time i looked different and felt the air of another planet far away from this room-world. it must have been a long time ago and i must have changed a lot, as i can only remember my early past darkly. my present, too, by the way, as i am blind. though from time to time i do hear quite a few things.

knife and fork alternately tap the first two bars of beethoven's fifth symphony on the tabletop.

the table :

my strength undoubtedly lies in feeling. i can feel everything that touches me — but when it lasts longer, the feeling gradually fades. injuries to my surface make me suffer : i gasp when scratched, scream when beaten, whimper when drilled into, and sawdust pours painfully from my insides. i cannot fly on my own, my legs are lame and make me immobile, and yet, according to revelation, the ability to swim has been granted me — having said that, until now i have been waiting in vain for such undeserved happiness. nevertheless i trust in my redeemer, the table of all tables, the sublime, highest table, of unnatural origin, enthroned above all tables, who judges them, both good and bad. he is the one who will reward my steadfastness, for he, table-god, stands at my right hand, risen from the firewood and through purgatory into the air. as he possesses the power of changing forms, he will turn me into a fish and thus on the night of judgment — i did confess to being blind — the grace of swimming will be poured upon me beyond this room-world of mine. sometimes, when the ground trembles, i hear the hollow murmur of the cellar, my underworld. it promises me that, one day, when the earth upon which this room-world stands begins to shake i will be able to walk, even if only from wall to wall. but i renounce the earth as nothing but a form of the seducer's delusion.

while the monologue continues, the knife begins to move and as if magically attracted slides around the plate to the side of the fork, which, recoiling coquettishly, turns sideways to it.

the table :

i believe in the water, a river in the kingdom of the blessed that will carry me away to another, better world, a world without walls and borders, where i will swim blissfully between octopuses and sharks. my faith gives me stability, that is why i stand here and am unable to do anything else — so long as fate doesn't knock me down in anger. but table-god is just in his goodness and leaves me standing in the dark, for patience and gentleness are mine, and i forgive the hardwood chairs their careless bumps or deliberate kicks, yes, as it is written, to the beater i also turn my other three sides.

the knife woos the fork's tines until she allows him to exploratively stroke alongside.

the lines become melodramatic to piano accompaniment.

the knife :

may i may i may i tell me please

the fork :

goodness already so pointy and ready to tease

the knife :

yeah if that is what you want want want

the fork :

you better cool down with your taunt taunt taunts

the knife :

some call me mack-the-knife
oh baby how i like to cut into flesh
when with the fork i am enmeshed
more than anything in this life

the fork :

a napkin will do for a white dress
but as candy to the knife's old eye
the decision to bare all and shine
is up to me, and nothing less

the knife :

slits slits
red-hot fits
with the tip
into the slit

the fork :

cut the schtick
and make it quick
there's space enough
in the slit
from the grip
up to the tip

the knife :

into the slit
with the tip
up to the grip
two sharp lips

the fork :

when i lie
or sit
when i stand
or flit

the knife :

into the slit
with the tip
yeah i'm quick
ain't no schtick

the fork :

just look at them wave
while bright drops upon them blaze
my slender tines they crave
to lap them up in praise

the fork has turned onto its back. with its tip, from the opposite side, the

knife probes the tines until it finds the opening in the middle, slips up to the handle and both begin to move rhythmically up and down (back and forth) to the music.
the fork :

knife oh knife do cut me more
your sharpness makes me soar soar soar
and knife dear knife if you're so pointy
don't ask what to cut oh so coyly

in the meantime the spoon has risen, and is now standing upright on the other side of the plate and watching the two of them from the inside.
the spoon :

a fresh cut's how it all begins
then on it goes all outs and ins
from the tip right up to the grip
with a swing — that's the trick

change of position : the knife draws a semicircle around its own axis, the fork lies down, facing the knife expectantly, and the knife, now lying sideways as well, slips between the aforementioned middle tines.
the knife :

as you know
it's all so
factual
practical

the fork :

so very practical
and oh how tactile

change of position : the fork turns its curved side towards the knife, the knife approaches from behind.
the fork :

oh how very tactile
and ever so tactical

the knife :

i cut and cut and cut

cutting for me is never enough
cutting whatever the fork might hold
cutting my way across the globe

the spoon :

there sure is a lot to hear and to see
and ever so gleeful, not to mention free

the teaspoon bobs up a bit several times, as if it also wanted to sit up but stops in the slightly raised position, since it can't get any higher.

teaspoon :

i hear what i like to hear
but hidden so that i don't appear
of course i'd also like to see
i mean at least to some degree
who wouldn't understand me

it tries again but does not get any higher.

the spoon to the teaspoon :

be good you
you are still too small
for that jump
into happiness's thrall
the plate's too big
and the soup's too hot
to thine own self be true
what you don't know won't hurt you

change of position : knife and fork are now doing it standing up, without having separated from one position to the other. at the beginning hardly noticeable, but from now on increasingly so the table drawer opens and closes (to the audience) to the rhythm of the music : opens and closes, opens and closes, opens and closes . . .

the fork :

oh so sharp sharp sharp i want you entire

the knife :

whatever and always you require require require

the fork :

do let me know when you spill spill spill

the knife :

whenever it is you so will will will

standing up, the spoon teeters (back and forth).

teaspoon :

goodness what an itch
i swear it's reaching fever pitch

the spoon :

the sight alone'll make you hot
and break into a sweat right on the spot
i can't sit still a second longer
and the soup itself can't be much stronger

the knife :

yes i think it will be soon indeed

the fork :

oh how good that sounds to me

the knife :

yes now it's time it's true

the fork :

oh and i am really ready too

the spoon begins to rotate around its own axis.

the spoon :

now all and sundry seem spellbound
everything's spinning and turning round
knife fork spoon fork
quick goes the soup into the gorge

the soup excited (prose breaks from the rhythm) :

i am the soup
and want to be spooned!

the fork :

wei wa wa wa wa wa wa wa

the knife, inserting to the fork's fourth "wa"

yea ssa ssa ssa

both with decreasing volume :

blah blah blah blah blah blah blah blah
blah blah blah blah blah blah blah blah

the spoon, to the last eight "blahs" :

yeah yeah yeah there you go — there!

the spoon has swung up over the table and is clapping at the "there!" with full force into the soup plate, that the soup spills over (the plate breaks?). knife and fork separate. everything remains motionless on the dripping tabletop, only a bit of whipped cream dribbles out of the half-open table drawer.

or : the table has started to bob along more and more violently with the "wei wa wa" until with the "there!" everything slides down and the plates shatter (in front of the first row of spectators).

after a few moments of silence, in the tone in which it began (slightly slowed down by the slightly distorted tape speed), the table brings its monologue to a close :

blameless i am for what takes place upon me. an indecent wetness may sprinkle down from time to time, but its origins lie not with me. and when into me it seeps, i hardly dare to enjoy the refreshment, but sigh tearfully instead for dryness to come as soon as possible and the brush of punishment to rub me, and the rag of forgiveness to scrub and scour me until once again i shine in the old godly cleanliness of accustomed table manners.

lights out.

MUSIK ZUM "BESTECKSTÜCK" (1993) (12.–14. NOV.)

s. 3

welle tropfen blinken um sie aufzutrinken
G:
messer messer schneide messer schärfer
frag nicht was man schneiden darf
L: frischgeschliffen fängt es an schneidig geht es dann voran von der spitze bis zum griff
M: alles ist wie ihr wisst faktisch praktisch
G: ach so praktisch
und so haptisch
G: (y) ach wie haptisch (y) und ganz taktisch M: schneiden schneiden immer zu

schneiden ohne rast und ruh
schneiden was die gabel hält
schneiden durch die ganze welt
ich höre was ich gerne höre
war versteckt dass ich nicht störe
gerne würde
ich auch sehen
das wird jeder gut verstehen
wer will das nicht
auch was sehen
suppe ist für dich zu heiss
nach
du bist so scharf scharf scharf

kann nicht länger stille sitzen
suppe spritzen
ja jetzt wird es richtig bunt
messer gabel löffel gabel

note to "cutlery play"

writing theatrical pieces specifically for objects (of daily use) was something i had been planning for a long time. it seemed to me to be a contemporary corollary to the traditional puppet theater, something which — together with shadow play — has always fascinated me. such thoughts had also been inspired by the first attempts at a mechanical theater at the bauhausbühne (kurt schmidt) as well as in the soviet union of the 1920s (el lissitzky : *victory over the sun*). in a 1962 manifesto-like survey considering perspectives for a new theater ("foundations of a new theater") i wrote :

> "in the 'puppet theater' the performers are not self-acting people (individuals) but manipulated (moveable) objects (materials). obvious : the material no longer represents anything (puppets) but signifies itself (in the form of objects). result : a pure theater of objects.
> objects : natural objects, objects of daily use and aesthetic (art-) objects.
> the objects can move (mechanically or by trick) or be moved (visibly). they are 'situated,' they correspond somewhat to what one used to call 'decoration.' both real (unmodified) objects and enlarged, scaled down, deformed and (in their use) defamiliarized objects can be used.
> the objects do not simply function as incidental props but have meaning in themselves as elements of action."

in 1966 i created the play "ob-jects" in which objects of an extremely reduced "set" were placed into an atmospheric relationship throughout five constellations ("acts") with four different musical quotations, the point of which was to suggest a kind of rudimentary plot (premiere 1966 at the "forum theater" on kurfürstendamm in berlin). my reduced piece "the ring" is from the same year — you might call it a marital tragicomedy :

"curtain rises.
on the floor of the stage a wedding band.
curtain falls."

it was only in 1993, inspired by the "julia reicherts kabinetttheater," that i returned to the idea of a "theater of objects" and wrote a short piece accompanied by piano for a fork, a knife, a table, and a teaspoon, as well as a full soup plate, all acting in relation to a table soliloquizing at the beginning and end : the "cutlery play."

gerhard rühm

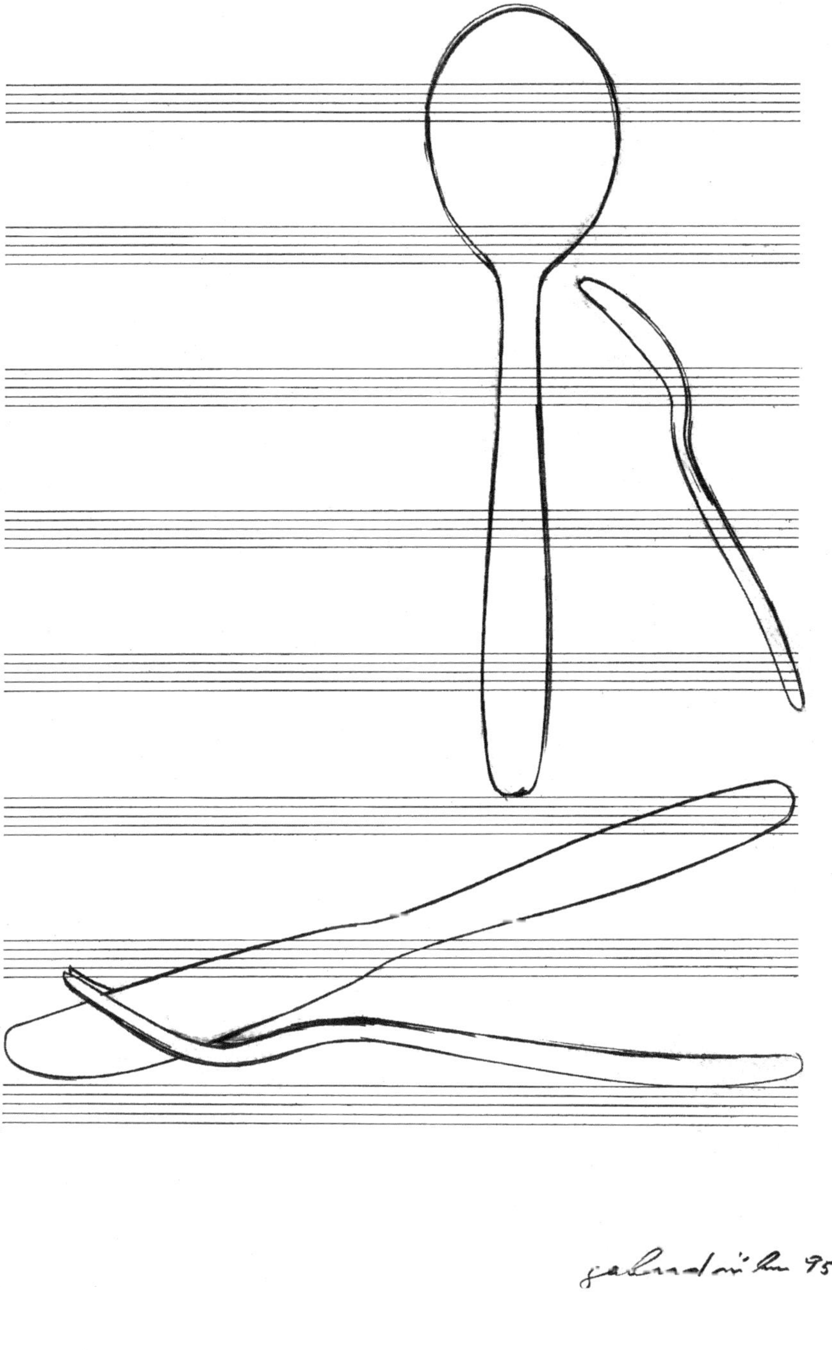

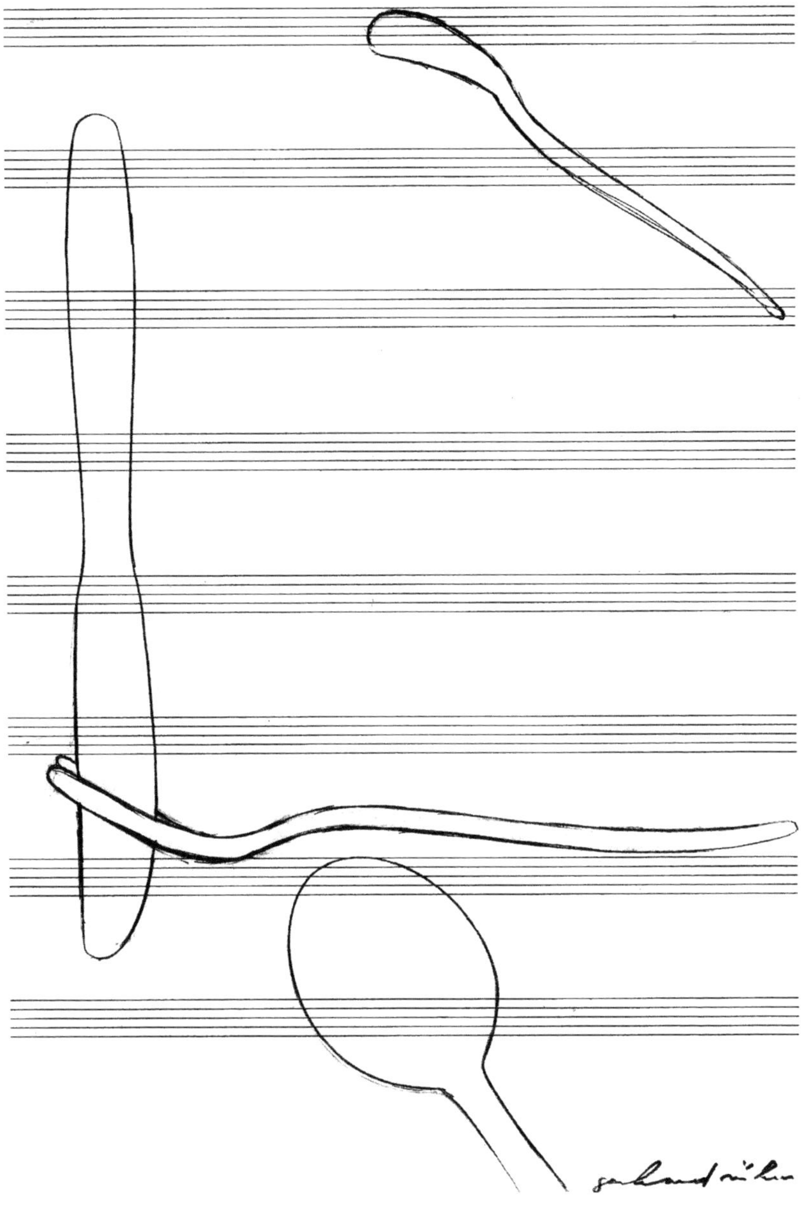
gerhard rühm 95

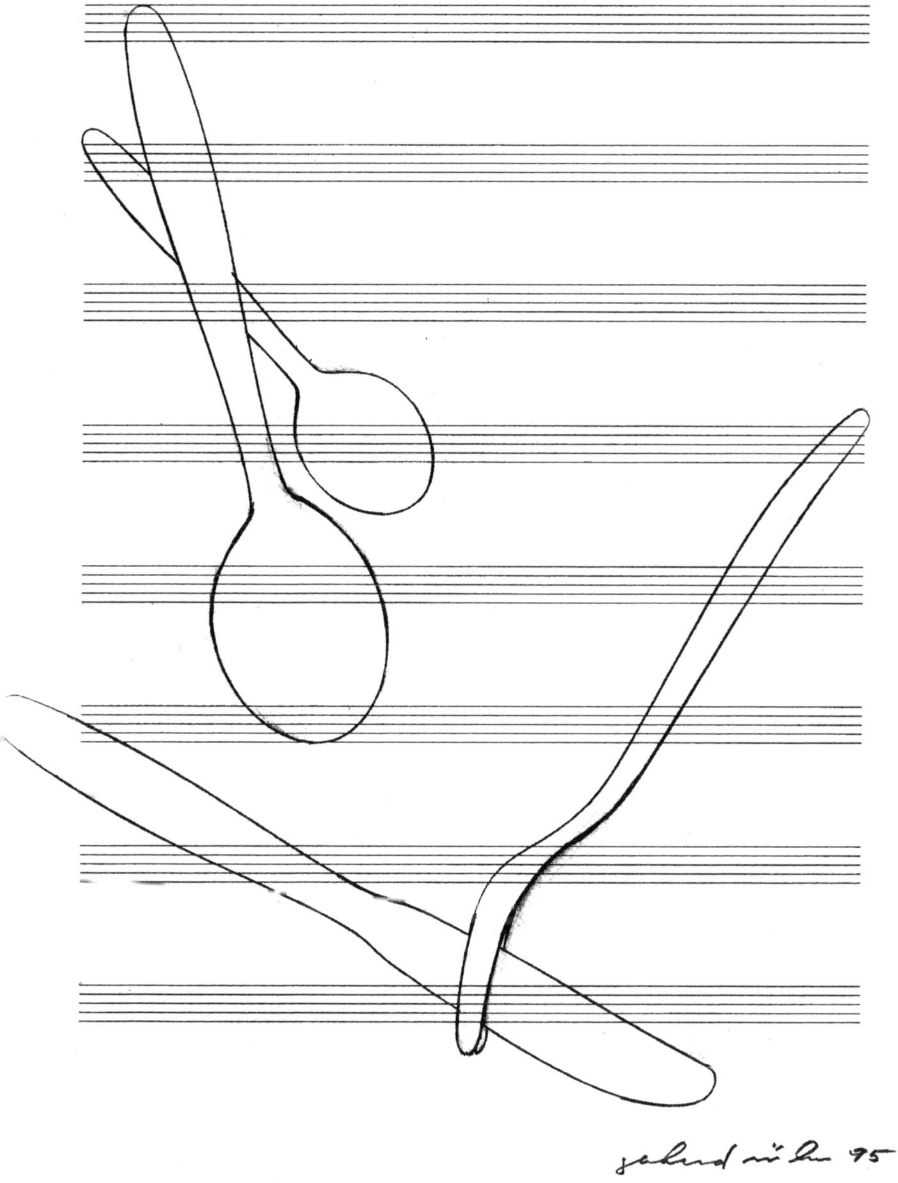

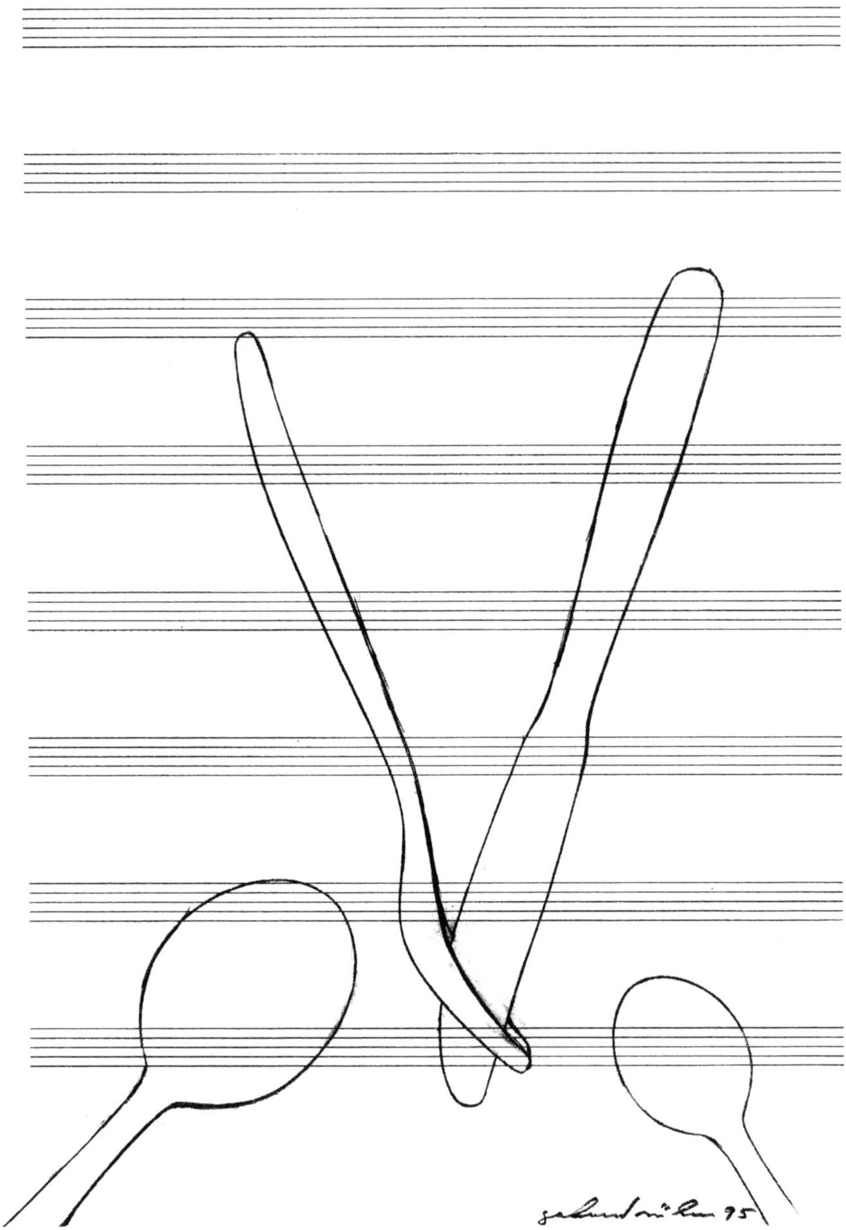

golden wedding

a puppet show with music

spoken duet

he : where have you
squirreled away my pills?
she : would you give me a sec?
i need to find my specs!
he : you have so many pairs,
which ones do you want?
the small-print ones for which
your hands were on the hunt?
she : no time to read the paper!
he : so, it's time to sweep instead?
she : no, pinhead, the room's already done.
he : well, no offense, hon',
this dust makes it look like a tomb!
she : for god's sake, would you
give me my specs at last?
he : you have so many pairs,
which ones do you want?
you want to have a look in the box
the one right there in front?
she : i'd like to see, you ass,
how old you've become!
he : for god's sake, give me
my pills instead!
she : you have so many pills,
out of their boxes they spill,
which do you want, mister?
the ones for your gut?
go on, be up front!
or the ones for your ticker?

he : you shouldn't play with me!
she : you have so many pills,
so which ones do you want?!
he : you know, the ones
i want every night!
she : hundreds of pills
out of their boxes they spill!
which ones do you want?
the ones for your head?
should i hit the package up?
or the ones for your gut?
(of which i've become quite fond)
he : all i want's the pill
that bacilli will kill.
she : what on earth do you mean?
they can't at all be seen!
he : not with the naked eye,
no, not even in the light.
she : it's specs the pills seem to need
or else the bacilli may breed!
he : why are you talking so much?
have you gone soft?
she : i've said it from the start
i've got to have my specs!
he : goddamn! you're just too blind
to find my pills this time,
so give me a ciggie instead
before i head off to bed.

plot

scenically, the themes of "pills" and "glasses" can be exploited to the full. even the lighting of the cigarette can be done, as a warning sign, with an exaggerated flame — "he" is still sitting at the dining table.

after several drags, "he" gets up to go and lie down, still dressed, on one of the marital beds which are along the righthand wall precisely for this reason. in the meanwhile "she" gets ready for her night's rest. he falls asleep, the still smoldering cigarette slips from his open mouth, the bedding catches fire and quickly bursts into flame. as soon as "she" notices it, "she" is shocked : with her hands against her heart, she falls over backwards dead.
from a trapdoor the devil appears and drags "him" (together with the burning bed?) to hell. on the ceiling (from the rigging) white clouds appear from which a little angel appears to haul "her" up into heaven. after a short period of silence a door opens in the middle of the backdrop and "he" comes onstage in reverse. his hair is disheveled, his clothes torn. more limping than walking "he" reaches the center of the stage and sits down, always with his back to the audience, where he remains motionless. while the following "swansong" is intoned, the stage grows darker and darker until the lights go out completely.

swansong

beyond the stage two voices ("he" and "she") in harmony, muffled, almost whispering, in a litany-like, expressionless tone :

pills forgotten
glasses forgotten
newspaper forgotten
broom forgotten
dust forgotten
television forgotten
boxes forgotten
furniture forgotten
rooms forgotten
lights forgotten
rivers forgotten
trees forgotten

clouds forgotten
animals forgotten
flowers forgotten
gardens forgotten
cities forgotten
streets forgotten
places forgotten
paths forgotten
parents forgotten
childhood forgotten
youth forgotten
friends forgotten
women forgotten
men forgotten
names forgotten
words forgotten

♩ ca 54
er: wo
hast du denn im stillen ver- räumt mir meine pillen? sie: ich brauch, um gottes willen, zum
suchen meine brillen! er: du hast so vielen brillen, welche tust du
willen? die für das klein ge- druckte, nach dem die hand schon zuckte? sie: nicht zeit zum zeitung
lesen! er: also für den besen? sie: der ist schon dran ge- wesen. er: aber, mit ver-

staub, über-all liegt staub! sie: gib mir, um gottes willen, endlich meine
brillen! er: du hast so vielen brillen, welche tust du willen? zum glotzen in die
kiste, die ich so gern vermisste? sie: sehn will ich, biga-mist, wie du ge-altert
bist! er: gib, um gottes willen, mir lieber meine pillen! sie: du hast so vielen
pillen, die aus den schachteln quillen, welche willst du willen? die gegen deinen
magen? du musst es mir schon sagen! die gegen deinen herzen? er: du sollst nicht mit mi
scherzen! sie: du hast so vielen pillen, nun, welche willst du willen? er: du weisst doch, welche

pillen ich jeden abend willen!
etwas breiter
dim.
poco rit.
a tempo
pp
sie: aus den schachteln quillen doch hunderte von
pillen! welche tust du willen? die gegen deinen köpfen, soll ich die schachtel
mp
schröpfen? die gegen deine därme, für die ich wenig schwärme! er: ich willen nur die
p
mf
pillen, die bazillen killen. sie: wer soll das verstehen? die kann man doch nicht
pp
sehen! er: mit blossen augen nicht, selbst nicht bei tages-licht. sie: die pillen brauchen
p
pp
brillen beim killen der ba- zillen! er: was redest du so vielen?! bist du schon ganz de-
mf

bilen?? sie von anfang hab ich sagen, ich müssen brillen tragen! er: bist du, verdammt!, zu blinden, die
pillen mir zu finden, denn gib mir ziga- retten, be- vor ich geh zu betten.
a tempo
poco rit.
dim.
(das bett fängt feuer)

(der teufel holt "ihn")
mp
mf cresc..
dim.
f
cresc..
dim.
poco dim.
ff
(ein engel holt "sie")
pp
(tür im hintergrund öffnet sich, "er" tritt im
rückwärtsgang auf, setzt sich)
er + sie: pillen vergessen, brillen vergessen, zeitung vergessen,
mit dämpfer

besen vergessen, staubvergessen, fernsehn vergessen, schachteln vergessen, möbelvergessen, räume verg., lichter verg.,
(bühne wird immer dunkler)
flüsse verg., bäume verg., wolken verg., tiere verg., blumen verg., gärten verg., städte verg.,
strassen verg., orte verg., wege verg., eltern verg., kindheit verg., jugend verg., freunde verg.,
frauen verg., männer verg., namen verg., worte vergessen . . .
(totale finsternis)
(vorhang langsam zu)
JUNI 2001

chamber play for brooms

a perpetuum mobile for cleaning props

a broom closet in somewhat distorted perspective : the two side walls run diagonally toward a very shortened back wall where a small barred window lets in sparse daylight. beneath it there is a tear-off calendar which – in easily readable size – only displays the names of the days of the week : "monday" on the first sheet. a long-handled broom leans in the corner. attached to the right wall is a shelf containing various cleaning products, next to it a duster. leaning against the left wall is a three-step ladder, next to it a hand broom and a shovel hanging close to the floor. front left a (smaller) trash can.

the music starts with the piano part (A), at the same time the duster comes off the wall and sweeps the shelf, creating a lot of dust.
once the piano part ends, a hand appears to tear off "monday" with a technically amplified ripping sound – darkness.
we hear vocal part (B) with the text :

> yesterday cleaned bright and early,
> and today already everything's so dirty.
> sure didn't help that much,
> here again now with broom and brush.

then the lighting as before. on the calendar sheet : "tuesday." to piano part (A), the hand broom now sweeps the steps of the stepladder (each step two beats long), creating a lot of dust. once again the hand appears at the end of the piano part and rips off "tuesday." darkness. repetition of vocal part (B).
light. "wednesday." accompanying piano part (A) the long-handled broom sweeps the floor – it's dusty! – and after the sustained final chord of the piano passage sweeps the dust onto the shovel, which dumps it into the trash can. "wednesday" is torn off. darkness. vocal part (B) follows.

the whole thing is repeated with the calendar sheets "thursday," "friday," "saturday."
in the darkness after "saturday" is torn off we hear the following two lines :

always so much to wipe, sweep and wax
today at last we can relax.

while everything is still in darkness the moon drifts into the window, producing a silver, unreal light. twelve strokes of a distant church bell. to the sounds of a celesta's "dream waltz" the objects leave their places and dance weightlessly around the room. once the music ends, in the short moment of silence we hear the stroke of "one" and immediately everything is back in place. even the moon has disappeared, and darkness reigns.

then straightaway the usual illumination. the calendar shows "monday." up to and including "wednesday," everything repeats as it did at the beginning. with a threefold

and so on

the chamber play ends in darkness. after a short pause for reflection, houselights.

MUSIK ZUM "BESENKAMMERSPIEL" für klavier und celesta

TRAUMWALZER celesta (register)
♩= 108
p
poco rit...
rit...

erotic pantomimes

delilah and samson
or
the magical triangle

in front of the curtain on the left, a piano. a singer and répétiteur appear and perform schubert's goethe lied "versunken" in the following adaptation :

dense frizzy curls the pudenda below! –
and can i take hold of such thick hair
with lusty hands, back and forth with flair,
o then i feel healthy from the bottom of my heart.
and when with open mouth i kiss those breasts, that navel,
then forever and again i'm raw, if able.
the five-toothed comb, where should it stop;
back already it has gone to those locks.
nor does the ear care to be cast aside,
here flesh rubs flesh, moist skin glides,
so tender in play, full of love we writhe!
and up and down we ascend and descend
this frizzy little mound forever and ever amen!

after applause both walk off.
curtain rises.
a canopy bed in the middle of the stage.

scene 1

delilah and her bosom friend thirza.
thirza is trying to coax delilah into telling her the secret of her power over samson. delilah embarrassedly shakes her head. thirza doesn't let up and pesters delilah until she – under the seal of strictest confidence (index finger to her lips) – relents with a sigh and draws a triangle in the air, standing on its tip. thirza's uncomprehendingly questioning look. delilah gathers courage (she doesn't want to seem like a prude),

hikes up her skirt and points to her black-haired pubis : this is what always captivates samson.
a number girl with a sign prances along the stage from the right, stopping briefly halfway. in biblical letters we read :

THERE HATH NOT COME
A RAZOR UPON MY MONS.
IF I BE SHORN,
MY STRENGTH FROM ME IS GONE.

she leaves. from the left a revue girl with a blackboard (fashionable writing) :

THE MODERN WOMAN SHAVES OFF HER PUBIC HAIR!

thirza surreptitiously taps herself on the forehead : she has an idea. once again facing delilah, with the appropriate gestures she encourages her to follow such advice immediately — she would be happy to help her with the procedure. samson would surely welcome the change, and delilah's power over him could only grow.
delilah, noticeably unsettled, expresses doubts, which thirza eagerly tries to dispel. in vain. she decides to overwhelm delilah by acting quickly. she leaves the stage in a hurry to get the necessary utensils.
delilah tries to take advantage of her friend's absence to escape — but she's hesitated too long! thirza is already back, proudly brandishing a shaving set.
delilah is not exactly pleased. but her resistance wanes in the face of thirza's compelling thirst for action. defeated, she lets thirza put her in the required position and shave away. after the work is done, thirza performs an admiring pantomime in which she congratulates delilah on the allegedly so advantageous change, while delilah looks skeptically at her shorn self.

scene 2

samson's appearance. thirza scurries unnoticed behind a screen in the background while delilah quickly makes herself presentable.
samson expresses his desire to climb into the inviting canopy bed with

her. expressing surprise, delilah urges him to be patient. samson adopts an expectant attitude. delilah seductively removes her few articles of clothing and directs his gaze with a presenting gesture to her depilated mons. violently startled, samson backs away. icy disillusionment. reluctant shaking of the head, accompanied by a defensive hand movement. angry, samson turns away.
one hand over her genitalia, the other over her face, delilah rushes off distraught.

scene 3

thirza comes out of hiding. her lascivious movements immediately attract samson's attention.
music begins : "dance of the priestess of dagon" (finale of act 1) from the opera *samson and delilah* by camille saint-saëns in the composer's piano transcription. with a prolonged striptease, thirza captures the all too willing samson. with the final chord, the last veil is dropped : seeing the black-haired pubic triangle samson is electrified.
his lust is awakened anew. throwing off the cloak, he drops to his knees to kiss the magic triangle. now sitting on the edge of the bed, thirza triumphantly presses his head between her thighs with both hands and lets herself fall backwards.
lights out.

scene 4

music : the "bacchanale" (act 3, scene 2) from the same opera. on the darkened stage, samson and thirza make love. with the final *stretto* the scene becomes acoustically turbulent, too. a shared scream — the canopy bed collapses with a crash.
silence.

scene 5

light.
samson and thirza lie as if lifeless between the canopy bed's debris.

alarmed by the noise, delilah rushes back onstage in her bathrobe. for a moment she stands before of the situation in shock. suddenly, she taps herself on the forehead, beaming : now *she* has an idea.
she nimbly fetches the shaving implements and lines them up in front of the unconscious thirza. unexpectedly, the opportunity for revenge has come!
first she takes the scissors and trims thirza's pubic hair to short stubble, before shaving off the corners, leaving only two narrow middle strips. delilah straightens herself up and examines her work with obvious satisfaction.
samson slowly comes to, pushes the shattered wood aside, stretches and wobbily rises to his feet. horrified, he sees thirza's deformation. disgusted, he throws a shredded sheet over her body.
only now does he notice delilah, who can't suppress a mischievous smile. ruefully, he embraces delilah again — even though the two of them will have to be patient for a few more weeks. as the pianist plays the last eleven bars of the opera, the curtain falls.

pygmalion and galatea

the first 35 bars (*allegro spirituoso con brio*) of the overture to the comic-mythological opera *the beautiful galatea* by franz von suppé. curtain rises with the f sharp major chord (bar 36).
in the middle of the stage a riser-like couch faces the audience (the lower end to the right). spread with a white cloth whose outlines suggest a human figure lying beneath (knees bent upwards). on the floor diagonally in front of it sculptor's tools (chisel, hammer . . .). on a side wall, a folding chair.
after a pregnant silence pygmalion appears. he is wearing a dusty, formerly white work coat and sandals. he pauses indecisively before the riser (hand on chin), then sets up the folding chair and sits down (back to the audience). he thinks for a while, now and again whistling thoughtlessly the waltz motif of *the beautiful galatea* that will be heard later.
having come to a decision, with an elegant swing in the manner of a magician, he reveals galatea, stretched out as if in a painting. like a nude sculpture she remains motionless in a fixed position (head and shoulders on a wedge-shaped wooden support).
pygmalion pushes the chair to the side and takes a step back to have the precocious girl's body completely in his field of vision. hand flat before his eye, he covers individual parts, measures and compares proportions between his hands and spread fingers (thumb and forefinger) in the air. he then circles the riser and observes the figure from different angles — assisted by a spotlight, which tests changing shadow effects.
here and there pygmalion changes the position of an arm, a hand, the head — checks the effect several times from a distance. eventually he turns to the position of the legs : he shortens the angle of the raised left knee by carefully shifting the foot on top. moves the right outstretched leg to the front edge, examines it. slowly guides the foot over the edge

to the ground. continued adjustments at the opening of the thighs show the figure in an ever more provocative pose. throughout all of pygmalion's manipulations galatea must remain inanimate, like a mannequin, maintaining even the smallest change.
after a detailed inspection, pygmalion nods with satisfaction. he now lifts his work coat (his back to the audience), whose rapidly accelerating fluttering suggests : pygmalion is masturbating. moistened by his ejaculate, galatea comes to life. music : the 30 bars (*andante*) of the overture following the introduction. she lolls about, tentatively straightens up, looks childishly astonished at pygmalion — all according to a choreography adapted to the music. after the *andante* ending with a d-major chord in *fortissimo* there is a leap in the music to the *più moderato*. pygmalion gallantly grasps galatea's hand, pulls her to him, kisses her paternally on the mouth and dances with her around the riser — music : 17 measures (with upbeat) of the *più moderato*, then jump to the 5th measure (with upbeat) of the *allegro* (tempo I). in a large arc they both now spin offstage in waltz step.
at the final bars of the overture (*ancora più mosso*) the curtain quickly falls.

the bremen town musicians
a children's pantomime with animal noises

introductory remarks

the animals played by the four children are identified by characteristic attributes. for example, the donkey has long erect ears, the dog has a tail it can wag, the cat has whiskers sticking out, the rooster has a red-toothed cockscomb. the robbers, on the other hand, are played by four adults. they are wearing masks with the features of egomaniac types we know from the media, such as corrupt politicians, unscrupulous entrepreneurs, talentless show-business "stars." they remain silent throughout, even once they get frightened and run off.
it goes without saying that music is out of place here. whatever happens acoustically — apart from unavoidable background noise — is limited to the animal voices alone.

the donkey steps out in front of the curtain from the left and says tiredly:

e o.

with gestures that express his hunger, he trots to the center of the stage, where he sees the exhausted dog stretched out on the ground. as if stricken himself, he asks sympathetically :

o e?

the dog, sad :

bow-wow.

the donkey nudges him encouragingly and tells him to get up and come with him.

the dog gives two limp flaps of his tail, but then pulls himself together and agrees, resigned to his fate :

bow-wow.

almost keeping to their spot (to mimic a longer distance) they then wander off with the following duet :

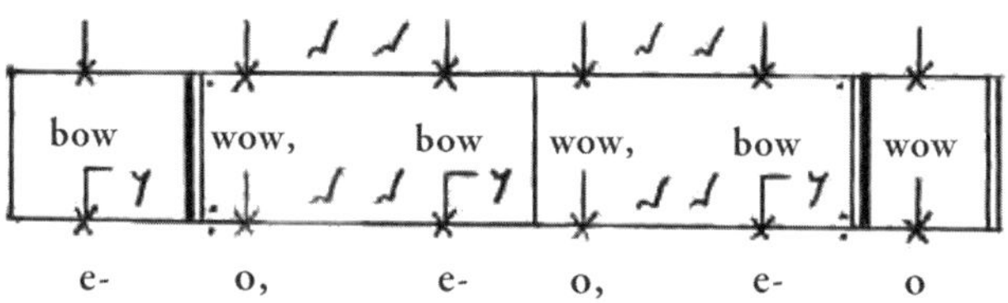

(repeat ad libitum)

in the meantime the cat has appeared from the left and after a plaintive

meow . . .

immediately following her first step crouches down on crossed legs — naturally, the cat is a female.

after having made sure someone is there with binoculars (rounded hands in front of their eyes), the donkey and the dog turn around and walk toward the cat. at an appropriate distance (but not too far away) they stop, bow and take a closer look.

the dog, worried :

ow ow . . . ?

as the cat sighs only once with a muffled "m," the dog and donkey become more insistent :

ow ow??

e – o??   (both together)

the cat responds apathetically with the counter question :

owem?

dog and donkey, even more emphatically :

bow-wow, bow-wow!

e – o, e – o!   (both together)

both indicate to her to join them.

still a bit coy, but urged on by the inviting gestures, the cat finally rises. on the dog's arm with the donkey behind them they set off once again singing the following terzetto :

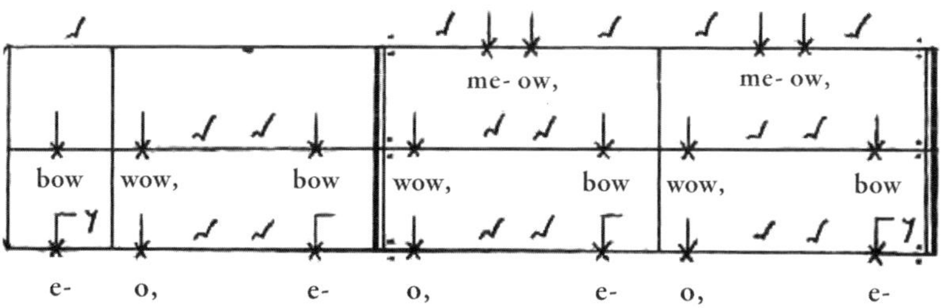

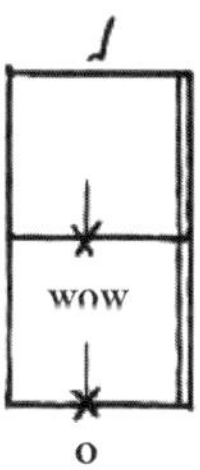

(repeat ad libitum)

just before the three unexpected comrades reach the exit stage right, from the left, still behind the curtain, we hear a pitifully breathless

cock-a-doodle-doo!!

the three of them turn around, momentarily startled.

the rooster — a little squirt — desperately flapping his wings (hands), stumbles onstage from the left and immediately falls over from excitement and exhaustion.

the cat, dog and donkey, visibly more lively as a group, hurry — each with their own characteristic movements — to the rooster's aid. having reached him, one after the other they try to calm him down :

meow,

bow-wow,

e' o.

the rooster rubs his neck fiercely, as if he had already been nicked by the butcher's knife. frightened :

cock-a-doodle-doo . . . ! (repeat ad libitum)

cat, dog and donkey, soothingly :

meow,

bow-wow,

e' o.

the rooster, gradually catching on (diminuendo) :

cock-a-doodle-doo . . .

small pause of general reflection.

first the cat, with an inviting gesture, gives the rooster to understand to join them :

owem . . .?!

the dog immediately agrees :

ow ow?!

and the donkey, too, affirms in a whimsical way (like "come along!") :

o e!!

the rooster, moved, gladly shows himself ready :

cock-a-doodle-doo, cock-a-doodle-doo.

the donkey helps the wing-beating rooster up in a comradely fashion, grasps him around the shoulder and follows in the cat's footsteps, who has already set off on the gallant arm of the dog.

the four, one pair behind the other, march quietly, but decisively, along the proscenium toward the exit stage right, now (as promised all along!) singing the following hiking song as a quartet :

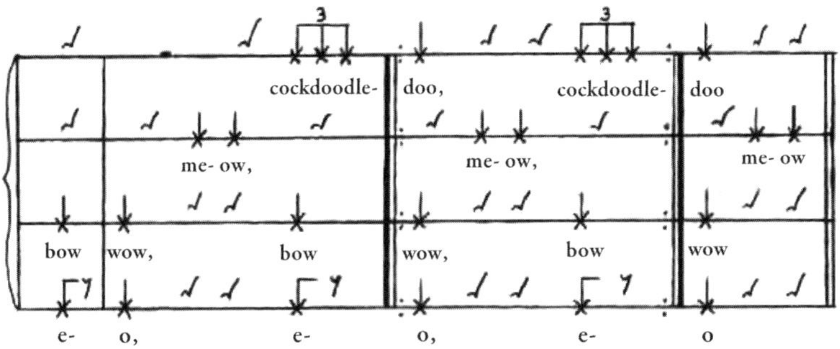

once the four have left the stage for a few beats we can still hear their voices which — as if moving away — quickly become quieter and fade away.

the curtain rises. under pale stage lighting an illuminated table around which four shady looking characters are seated. in front of each of them a plate of dumplings and a stein of beer. greedily they eat and drink — but their joy is short-lived.
suddenly, a spotlight illuminates the group of animals that had positioned itself stage right before the curtain rose : the rooster on the cat's shoulder, the cat on the dog's, and the dog on the donkey's back. in chorus they scream a frightful :

cock-a-doodle-doo!!!
me- ow!!!
bow-wow!!!
e- o!!!

the table group — at first frozen with fright — takes off in panic, chased by the donkey, dog, cat and rooster.
once the field is cleared, the four animals nod to one another in satisfaction and happily sit down around the table to continue the interrupted meal. before they satisfy their hunger, however, they sing a festive closing song :

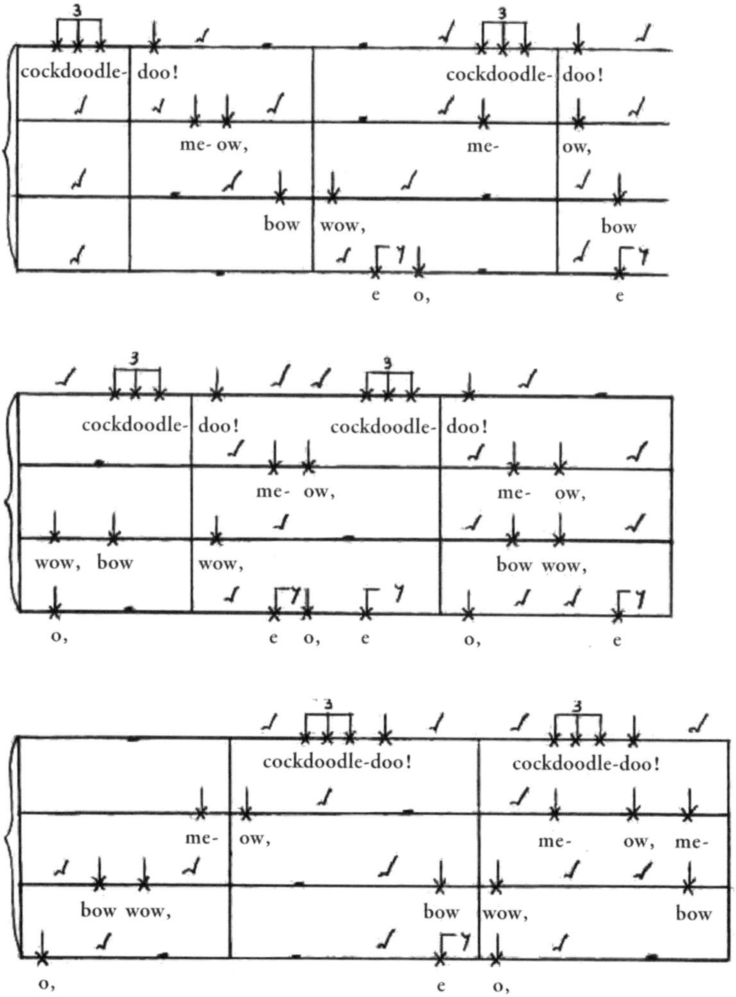
cockdoodle- doo! cockdoodle- doo!
me- ow, me- ow,
bow wow, bow
e o, e
cockdoodle- doo! cockdoodle- doo!
me- ow, me- ow,
wow, bow wow, bow wow,
o, e o, e o, e
cockdoodle-doo! cockdoodle-doo!
me- ow, me- ow, me-
bow wow, bow wow, bow
o, e o,

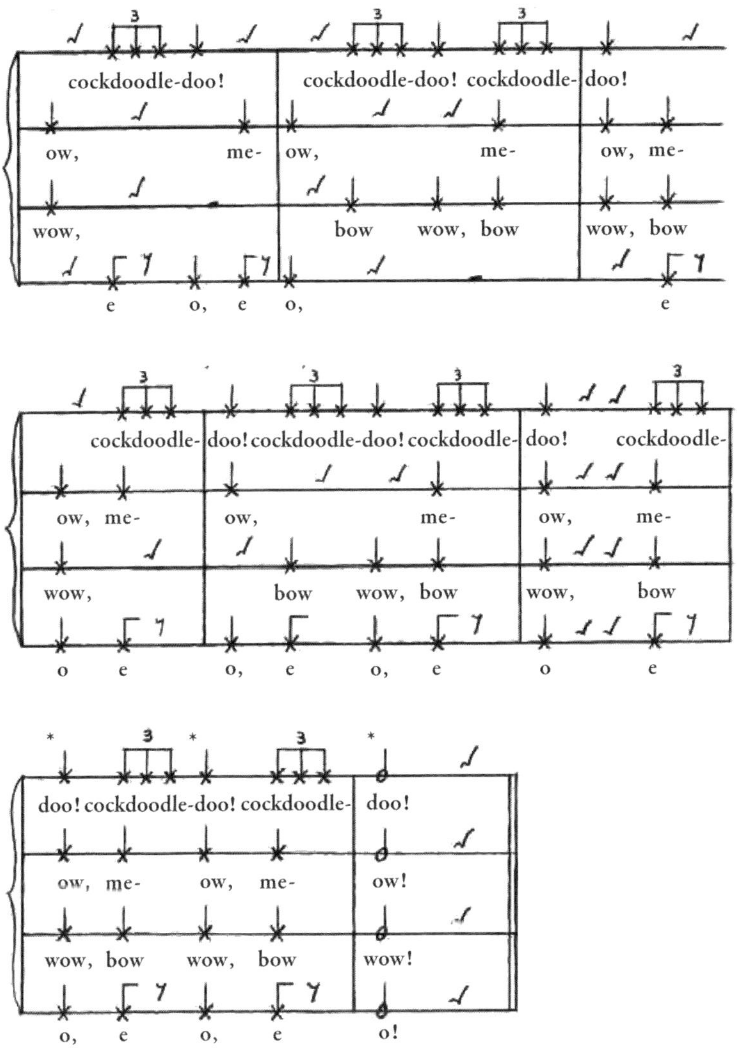

*at each of these points the donkey, dog, cat, and rooster can strike the steins and plates with their knives and forks.

curtain falls.

(2004)

pompes funèbres meyerbeer
a teichoscopic playlet

scene one

the curtain rises.
onstage we see a parisian living room in the style of the eighteen-sixties. in the background a window with a drape and curtains divided into two. next to it a side table with various objects. on the right, a door in a free-standing backdrop with flowered wallpaper. on the left, on a similarly patterned wall bordering the stage, a chaise longue. subdued daylight.

a young woman is resting on the chaise longue. her husband is sitting at the little table, cleaning a pair of opera glasses. both are wearing bourgeois home clothes, as was customary in meyerbeer's time. if possible the conversation in the first scene should be conducted in french while the original german version can be read in synchronous overtitles above the stage.

she, after a few minutes of silence :
do let in a bit of fresh air, please!

he : gladly.

he pulls the drape to the side and opens a casement. from "outside" the sound of a blackbird drifts in.

she, having grown attentive :
do you hear . . . ?!

he, in an unintentionally restrained voice :

. . . a blackbird.

he casts a glance out the window and apparently notices something that arouses his interest. during the following the blackbird's song slowly recedes into the background and is soon only audible intermittently, while he continues to lean on the windowsill and look out curiously.

she, as he cannot seem to turn away from what he sees :

what is happening outside that is so interesting?

he : a large crowd of people has gathered on the champs élysées . . . many are very smartly dressed . . . . among them deputies from theaters and academies, singing societies . . . obviously all in expectation of an important event . . . . in front of the rue montaigne there's a six-horse black-covered court coach, decorated with laurel wreaths . . . . the lord steward has just stepped out of the carriage and paused in military posture . . . all eyes are glued to the open gate of the corner house on rue montaigne . . . . two uniformed servants with parade wreaths step out of the house . . . behind them you can now see a coffin — it is wrapped in a black velvet blanket embroidered with white stars and richly laden with immortelle wreaths and bouquets of flowers . . . flanked by torchbearers . . . . with measured steps and bowed heads the coffin is being brought to the hearse . . .

she, with feigned interest :

a state funeral . . . ?

he, turning to her briefly :

well, didn't meyerbeer die a few days ago . . . ?

she :   oh, true! giacamo meyerbeer!
she casually removes a pearl necklace from around her neck.

he, leaning out of the window again :
the hearse has slowly started to move.

at the word "move," the muffled beats of a large drum sound in the sustained rhythm of a funeral march :

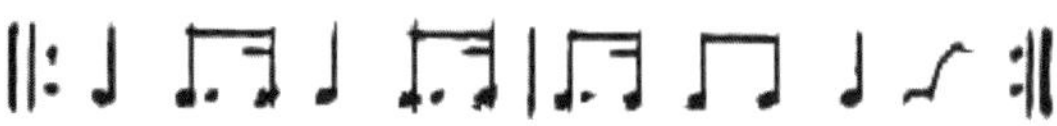

from the first repetition on, a muffled tam-tam beat accentuates the first beat of the two.

he :   the sappers of the national guard are in the lead, behind them the music corps of the grenadiers and the gendarmerie . . . a master of ceremonies is carrying a cushion — (he picks up the opera glasses from the side table) decorated with meyerbeer's numerous medals . . .

she, with a certain sympathy :
one less shining star!

she slips out of her velvet slippers and pushes them aside.

he :   a rabbi is holding the old testament in his hands . . . he is being followed by other rabbis and synagogue attendants . . . the dead man's relatives, mourners, dignitaries . . . members of the conservatory, the society of dramatic writers . . . the staff of the grand opera, the opéra-comique and the théâtre lyrique . . . deputations of the german choral societies "teutonik" and"liedertafel" — their banner inscriptions give them away.

he quickly looks back at her. she strips off her stockings and garters.

he continues his report, hesitating briefly :

seventeen, eighteen — no, twenty funeral carriages, plus several equipages, are following the procession at a walking pace . . . . an ever-growing crowd of silent mourners has joined the procession . . . a never-ending rearguard . . .

she, with a slightly ironic undertone :

all that you see . . . !

she takes off her dress, at which point she starts to attract his interest.

she, after a small pause for effect :

and now . . . ?

uncertain, he understands her remark as an invitation to report further :

just now the procession is moving through the avenue des champs-élysées . . . . it's reached place de la concorde . . . . a group of musicians is already waiting for them there . . .

she : are there any famous composers among them?

he reaches for the opera glasses again :

i think i recognize auber and, all the way up front, gounod . . .

she, smiling maliciously :

the great rival is dead!

he : from the rows of curious onlookers at the side of the street some women are hurrying toward the hearse . . . hastily throwing wreaths and flowers over the coffin.

while he speaks in an increasingly excited voice, she sheds her blouse in a deliberately relaxed manner. turning back into the room, he stares at her for a moment, obviously undecided whether he should leave the window just before the unusual spectacle outside has reached its destination.

she, coquettishly insistent :

go on, go on . . .

he : the funeral procession has reached the grands boulevards . . . it's now moving past the black-flagged opéra . . . crossing boulevard haussmann, turning into rue lafayette and moving toward gare du nord . . .

she, playfully :

toward gare du nord . . .

he : hundreds of thousands are crowded about in anticipation of the hearse — the station walls are emblazoned with the signs of opera titles *robert le diable, les huguenots, le prophète, l'étoile du nord* . . .

by now, as if it were from afar, the funeral march rhythm breaks off. a moment of silence. she unbuttons her bodice and throws it in with the other garments.

he, with his gaze swinging restlessly between her and what is happening outside :

the coffin has arrived! . . . the funeral cortège has stopped . . . in front of gare du nord's black-draped entrance there's a huge catafalque — high flames of the sacrificial fire! — what a spectacle!

she removes her panties as the last piece of clothing. at the same time a soft drum roll (a small drum) begins and increases steadily until the end of the scene.
naked now, she stretches herself out on the chaise longue while he hastily closes the window and draws the curtains. immediately dark.
the stage curtain falls, leaving only a narrow gap. during the change of scene, the song of a blackbird can be heard throughout the auditorium.

scene two
(metamorphosis)

the curtain rises.
the stage is bright as day. the song of the blackbird can be heard again from the open window. the locations of the props are the same as in the first scene, only the style has changed : we are in the present day. the wallpaper on the movable walls is a single color (light yellow), the chaise longue has been replaced by a couch, the old chair by a new one, the side table by a modern cd, cassette and radio combo. there is no drape and the curtains are simple and translucent. the characters are the same as in the previous scene but appear noticeably aged. the woman is wearing a light bathrobe, the man a normal robe.

she is resting casually on the couch and reading a book. after a few minutes, he enters the room through the door on the right.

he, as she does not react to his appearance :
what has you so engrossed over there?

she : you know — i'm still on the meyerbeer biography. i've just gotten to the part where they're transferring his body to berlin after all the pompous mourning ceremonies in paris, where, as you know, he died.

he, sitting down :

read it out loud!

she : In a final decree, Meyerbeer, who always harbored a great fear of being buried alive, demanded that his corpse, with bells on its hands and feet and closely guarded, remain in the bed in which he had died for four days, and only then be coffined and transferred to Berlin, where it was to be buried at his beloved mother's side. These instructions were followed exactly. It was not until Friday, May 6, that the coffin was led in the most magnificent funeral cortège to the Gare du Nord for further transport to Germany. At six in the evening the special train, in which the coffin, the deceased's family members, the director of the Opéra and the publisher Brandus had all been settled, left for the deceased's home country, via Belgium, reverently greeted along the way at many stations by deputations and funeral songs. In the Opéra in Paris, that same evening the 398th performance of *Les Huguenots* took place, after which fourth act, accompanied by the sounds of the prophet's march, the artists placed a wreath upon the bust of the immortalized. The coffin's transfer from Potsdamer Station in Berlin to Meyerbeer's apartment at Pariser Platz No. 6 was unobtrusive and silent. The official funeral was scheduled for Monday, May 9, at noon. After an internal ceremony in the house of mourning officially attended by Prince George of Prussia, delegates of the court, the ministries and public art institutions, as well as the envoys of France and Italy, at which the rabbi Dr. Joël, who had been called from Breslau, gave the memorial speech and a solo quartet from the opera performed several of Meyerbeer's songs, an impressive funeral procession was formed. In front, under the leadership of General Music Director Wieprecht, the united bands of all of Berlin's cavalry regiments (120 wind players with black-creped instruments), behind them the opera's delegation led, in the absence of the director, by Kapellmeister Taubert, followed by a simple hearse, in accordance with Jewish custom, which bears all in the same way without distinction of rank or wealth, surrounded by the twelve youngest members of the court orchestra bearing palms. Walking behind the body were Meyerbeer's relatives and the official deputations, including the director of the Opéra. The end of the train was formed by an endless line of carriages, led by the six-horse gala carriage of the royal house. An incalculable crowd filled the streets through which the procession passed. When it arrived by the linden trees before the opera house, a mighty black flag of mourning was raised and the opera choir, which had been placed on the ramp, sang a chorale. The singers then joined the procession which now made its way to the Jewish Cemetery by the Schönhauser Gate. In a black decorated hall, surrounded by an abundance of exotic plants, stood a catafalque upon which lay the coffin, covered with a black, silver-ornamented blanket, resplendent in a profusion of sumptuously blooming wreaths; six candles surrounded the coffin, six candelabras, the catafalque, and a chandelier casting its bright rays from the ceiling onto the coffin. Close by, on the same black pillows, lay the numerous medals of the deceased, next to which the royal Kapellmeister Taubert laid a white satin cushion with a laurel wreath. At the grave, surrounded by more than ten thousand mourners, Count Redern and Botho von Hülsen once again paid tribute to the man and the artist. The Singakademie said farewell with Meyerbeer's "Hymn of Thanksgiving" and his "Psalm 91," known as "Trost in Sterbensgefahr," which he had set to music in 1853. The envoy of the King of Württemberg addressed the dead Commander of the Order of the Crown as "Knight Meyerbeer," and then the eldest grandson said the Kaddish, the traditional prayer for the dead. While Dr. Joël "took up" a text from the Pentateuch, the coffin was lowered into

> the tomb. Up until then Meyerbeer's wife, Minna, had admirably maintained her stoic bearing, but now she sank to her knees, shaken by violent convulsions of weeping. The daughters picked her up and escorted her from the cemetery, which she never entered again.

apparently tired from reading aloud, she puts the book down, whereupon he rises, walks to the front of the stage and addresses the audience (in the meanwhile, the blackbird's song has subsided).

he, in an urbane and authoritative moderator-like manner (à la jürgen kesting) :

> let us treat ourselves to vasco de gama's wonderful aria "pays merveilleux" from the fourth act of *l'africaine*, meyerbeer's final opera.

he puts a cd in the player. both listen attentively to the music. when applause is heard at the end of the aria (from the cd), the curtain quickly falls.

(2007)

your fur coat, madame, is mine!
a playlet

a fur store. warm yellowish light. muted sweet music. a customer is trying on a fur coat, she looks at herself from all sides in the standing mirror, puts it down — still undecided — and spreads it over an upholstered armchair. she takes another model from the rack, slips into it briefly, hangs it back up — not quite right. she devotes more time to a third model, enjoying the wrap while posing seductively, turning back and forth before the mirror. eventually she puts the first coat back on the hanger, lays the one she has just tried on over the armchair instead in order to look at yet another one for comparison. at the moment she takes the fourth fur coat the following text is played from a loudspeaker. it is recited calmly and matter-of-factly. the customer, utterly preoccupied with choosing the right fur coat, takes no notice.

> one hundred million animals are killed annually worldwide for the fur industry. just under half of them are wild animals that have been bred specifically for fur production and only know captivity in a cramped cage. over the last few decades the production of fur has multiplied : this has been made possible by mass animal husbandry in confined spaces and the concomitant cheapening of the "commodity" as well as the development of new, mainly female, consumers. practically all the countries in the world are involved in this extreme cruelty to animals, which exclusively serves the satisfaction of vanity, whether producer or consumer.
>
> in addition to the farmed animals, there are about forty million free-living fur animals, which are "taken from nature," that is, caught, bludgeoned to death, strangled, shot or poisoned. in reality, however, the number is much higher, as only one third of

the captured animals can be used for fur production — the rest are considered refuse.
about ninety percent of fur-bearing animals are caught, primarily, in steel traps. when an animal steps onto the plate, the trap irons, which are equipped with a row of teeth, close. the trapped leg is severely injured, often even broken, and the animal desperately tries to get free. in the process, frantic with fear and pain, the animals cause even worse injuries to themselves, some even bite off their own legs to free themselves from the trap. death often comes only after days of agony.
other methods include hunting with a rifle and the use of poison bait or wire snares. in canada, thirty percent of fur-bearing animals are still caught with snares. this method is particularly cruel : if an animal gets caught in the trap by its head, it stands no chance of escape. the snare is constructed in such a way that it tightens with every movement and slowly strangles the animal.
to satisfy the increasing demand for the coveted hides more and more breeding farms have sprung up : minks, foxes, polecats, nutrias, chinchillas, and raccoons are now being produced on an industrial scale. thanks to the constant intensification of husbandry methods in smaller and smaller cages fur coats have gone from being a status symbol to being a mass-produced article for broad swaths of the population.
in mink and fox farms, up to ten thousand animals are crammed into cramped cages that do not protect them from the cold and wind. cold stimulates hair growth. the animals, which are sensitive to odors, must spend their lives in their own excrement. their mixed feed is simply smeared on the cage as a mushy lump. to reach it, the minks lick the rusty wire mesh. in the winter months, their tongues regularly freeze to the metal. the animals try to tear themselves away in panic, pieces of the tongue often remain stuck, sometimes the entire tongue is torn out of the mouth. with foxes, the animal least accustomed to being caged in groups, it

leads to increased aggressiveness and to abnormal behavior; they nibble on or even eat one another.

one of the most common epidemics in fur farms is botulism. in an outbreak, up to ninety percent of the animals die. there is no treatment. the infected minks gradually become paralyzed, they suffer from respiratory distress, their pupils dilate. eventually their bodies go limp, their paralyzed hind feet drag, and soon they can no longer even lift their heads. it can take days for death to deliver them.

minks in the wild take up to sixty minutes to mate, which is too long for breeders. since the male already discharges sperm at the beginning, breeders abruptly interrupt the mating act after only a few minutes by pulling the male out of the female, often resulting in the penis bone breaking. with chinchillas and rabbits, artificial insemination is also used. the sperm is extracted from the male animals by means of electroshock. electrodes are inserted into the rectum up to the sacrum and repeated electrical stimulation triggers the release of sperm. artificial insemination is also used with the very sensitive foxes. they are forced to become accustomed to masturbation at an early age and "trained" for mating season. for this purpose the animal is taken out with a gripper, fixed in a box that is open on one side and brought to ejaculation manually. the vixen is inseminated by means of a metal catheter shoved through the vagina into the uterus — a painful procedure, which is associated with enormous stress and is repeated up to four times per heat period. it is not uncommon for the probe to pierce the vagina, or for other serious injuries occur.

foxes are "harvested" at the age of seven months. this can be done in different ways : the animals are injected with a toxic solution, which only paralyzes the heart and respiratory muscles if the poison is immediately injected into the blood. because in most cases the animals fight back violently, the injection often

does not hit the heart directly, which can lead to twenty-five minutes of death throes. the most common and cruelest way of killing foxes and minks is electrocution. one electrode is clamped to the animal's snout, another is pushed into the anus. the electric shocks cause the animal to convulse in excruciating agony until death finally occurs after eight or more seconds. if the strength of the current is insufficient, some animals regain consciousness, and the procedure begins anew. if they are only paralyzed, they are skinned while fully conscious.
depending on the type of animal and the size of the coat, a fur coat costs the lives of between sixteen and one hundred and sixty animals :
sixteen foxes for one fox coat,
seventeen ocelots for one ocelot coat,
thirty nutrias for one nutria coat,
thirty-six unborn karakul lambs for one broad-tailed jacket,
forty raccoons for a raccoon coat,
sixty minks for a mink coat, and
one hundred and sixty chinchillas for a chinchilla coat.

toward the end of the report, there are several disturbing scraping, scratching and knocking sounds at the door to the store, which increase and grow into a frightening furioso with the last line. at the final word, the door bursts open with an explosive crash, at the same time the light changes to a flaming red. twenty-four nude, shaven-headed children come rushing in on all fours — frightened, the lady in fur flees to an armchair.
in chorus the intruders shout "MY FUR!" the following verbs, distributed among the twenty-four individual voices, are spoken seamlessly, one after the other.

MY NAKEDNESS (chorus)
feels (voice 1)
sighs (v. 2)

senses (v. 3)
glows (v. 4)
throbs (v. 5)
twitches (v. 6)
burns (v. 7)
freezes (v. 8)
MY NAKEDNESS (chorus)
aches (v. 9)
groans (v. 10)
pants (v. 11)
howls (v. 12)
wails (v. 13)
weeps (v. 14)
sobs (v. 15)
screams (v. 16)
MY NAKEDNESS (chorus)
moans (v. 17)
gasps (v. 18)
whimpers (v. 19)
whines (v. 20)
bleeds (v. 21)
fevers (v. 22)
shudders (v. 23)
suffers (v. 24)

abrupt change of light to a cold blue. the voices are now becoming more aggressive and louder, while the nude children crowd around the woman from all sides and try to pull off her fur coat.

MY FUR! (chorus)
scratches you (voice 1)
teases you (v. 2)
itches you (v. 3)
rubs you (v. 4)

grinds you (v. 5)
carves you (v. 6)
bites you (v. 7)
stings you (v. 8)
MY FUR! (chorus)
nips you (v. 9)
pinches you (v. 10)
squeezes you (v. 11)
stretches you (v. 12)
MY FUR! (chorus)
burns you (v. 13)
plagues you (v. 14)
torments you (v. 15)
punishes you (v. 16)
MY FUR! (chorus)
chafes you (v. 17)
tickles you (v. 18)
vexes you (v. 19)
torments you (v. 20)
MY FUR! (chorus)
tortures you (v. 21)
marks you (v. 22)
MY FUR! (chorus)
judges you (v. 23)
MY FUR! (chorus)
ostracizes you (v. 24)

the nude children tear off her fur coat. darkness.

(2007)

hero reads grillparzer / leander learns to swim

a classic love story

Whoever desires to learn the art of swimming must first learn how to bathe properly, i.e., get used to the water in order to become familiar with the wet element. Above all, the learner really should practice diving often and staying underwater for long periods of time.

let us assume that it's a sunday and we see a convent rising up before us. on the occasion of such and such an anniversary of the alleged resurrection of christ, that is, on a day in the month of may, a celebration is taking place in the convent's inner courtyard. among those present we have to imagine a strikingly attractive novice, lingering somewhat uncertainly in the background. her placement in a nunnery was probably not entirely voluntary.

attracted by the young woman's appearance a youth from the neighboring village approaches her in the hopes of cautiously making contact. soon an almost confidential conversation ensues, during which she reveals her name to him: "hero." without missing a beat he introduces himself as "leander." — should the reader find this a bit far-fetched it might help to keep in mind that this does not concern a real incident, but a poetic text. should we find this more acceptable, we may well assume that, in view of musaeus's epic, the youth, whose real name is of no importance here, spontaneously pretended to be leander, perhaps in the hope of arousing hero's interest all the more. and, in fact, she was indeed excited by the surprising coincidence of those two suggestive names in the form of living persons, especially as the young man made quite a winning impression. all the preconditions for a closer relationship between the two were thus happily initiated for the course of the evening. in the end, when saying goodbye, leander got her to promise to see him again the following sunday.

but how was he supposed to get into the otherwise carefully locked convent, which, moreover, was separated from his hometown by a wide, flowing river? the only way he could see was to swim across it under the cover of darkness. the non-swimmer leander therefore had to take swimming lessons as soon as possible. one week, he thought, and he'd be ready to dare the adventure. as hero's cell was on the lowest floor, she would put a candle in her window to let him know which room was hers and leave the window open between saturday and sunday so that he could enter.

MONDAY

Push off strongly from the wall of the pool, put your face to the water, place both your heels together, with the feet pointing outward and the toes curled toward your upper body, and now, real slowly, tuck in both your feet, and slowly embrace the water sideways, and without completely stretching your legs, kick against it swiftly while holding them together. This tempo is completed only once following each push-off; remain on the water as long as your breath allows.

With each tempo, there will be some initial rocking back and forth, but this will disappear with continued practice.

the encounter with leander had made her think of grillparzer's play *the waves of the sea and of love*, otherwise known as simply *hero and leander*. she'd been utterly unaware of it before, either as a book or a performance, all she knew was that it had to do with the titular couple's ill-fated love story. at lunchtime, she scurried to the convent library, which was where she hoped to find a copy. and was in luck: under the letter "g" on the shelf she really did find an edition of grillparzer's works, the sixth part of which contained the title she was looking for. she disappeared unnoticed into her cell with the volume, where she immediately began to read.

ACT I

The outer court of the Temple of Aphrodite at Sestus. Across the center of the stage is a row of pillars at considerable intervals, a part of the peristyle. At the rear is the temple itself to which a flight of steps leads up. Toward the front, at the right, stands a statue of Eros; at the left, one of Hymanaeus.

Early morning.

Hero comes out of the temple and descends the steps; she has a small basket of flowers on one arm.

HERO So far, so good. I see the Temple's ready.
With myrtle vines and roses richly strewn
It bides the time until the festival.
And it's for me the festival is held!

quickly tired of grillparzer's somewhat stilted verse, she set the book down with the intention of finishing at least the first act later that night.

TUESDAY

If in the previous exercises you have achieved the proper calmness, the movements begin with the hands. These lie 4-5 cm under the surface of the water, with the fingers, unwebbed as they are, always closed to offer more resistance. To see how this works, stand in the water and press down with your palm, your fingers spread. After that, press down with your palm, your fingers closed. You will notice that the resistance of the water is much less in the former case than in the latter.

in the morning, more out of a sense of duty than any real interest, she picked up the book again and began with the second act.

ACT II

Grove of the Temple at Sestus. At the left, toward the rear, a bench with shrubbery around it

NAUKLEROS *(enters left)*
Leander, come; and hurry a little, please.

LEANDER *(appearing on the same side)*
I'm coming, see.

NAUKLEROS So quickly? Who'd believe it?
How long must I still lead you, tell me now,
For some misdeed at present quite unknown
And uncommitted, too, like the boy who guides
A blind man through the streets? How long must I
Still lead you through these cheerful crowded towns
From feast to feast, from marketplace to shrine,
In hope that somewhere you'll regain your spirits?

and yet she didn't get beyond these first lines today either. when she had trouble falling asleep — something quite unusual for her — did she read this act through to the end.

WEDNESDAY

Now come the most difficult exercises, namely, those with the hands and feet together. For this first attempt it is better to have two people. One person should be halfway in the water, with a hand under the other's chest. Once again, the learner, that is, you, pushes firmly off from the side of the pool, remains stretched out for a few seconds on the surface of the water, heels together, feet outward and with the toes pointing toward the upper part of the body. Again, your face must be resting in the water. Then slowly begin to make strokes with both hands. While slowly pushing your hands about ½ meter sideways you must also slowly pull in both feet. Then bring your hands in front of your chin and push them forward. When your hands are out in front, step sideways against the water and kick quickly and firmly. Propelled forward, you must remain still and stretched out on the water for as long as you can hold your breath. Once these tempos — with your face underwater — have been practiced long enough, real swimming begins.

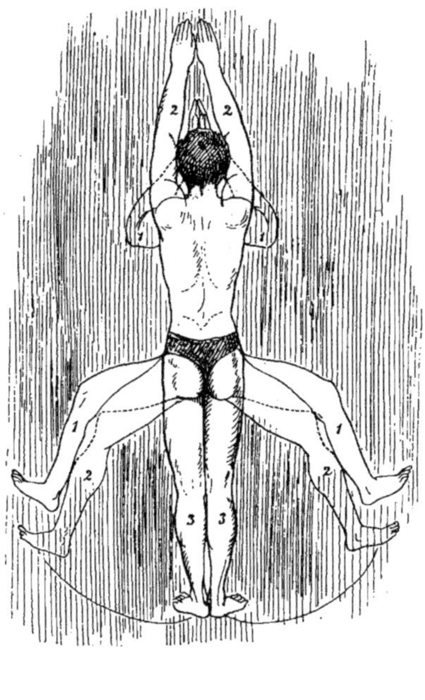

the third act didn't go any better than the second act the day before.

ACT III

Room in Hero's tower. At the right rear, in a deep embrasure, a bay-window to which several broad steps lead up; beside it is a tall lamp-stand: toward the left rear is a narrow door leading to the main hallway; right, halfway back, is a second door closed by a curtain; right front is a table, beside it a low-backed chair.

After the curtain rises, a servant enters bearing a lamp in his up-raised hand; he sets it on the lamp-stand and goes out; immediately after, enter the High Priest and Hero, who wears her cloak as at the end of Act I.

PRIEST The duties of your holy office have been
Fulfilled, and night draws near. Come to your house,
Your home henceforth, the priestess' quiet dwelling.

HERO *(gazes about her)*
Here; it is here.

After pushing off, slowly sweep your hands around with a downward movement. Take a breath, slowly pull up your feet and push your hands forward, then let your legs grasp the water and kick your feet firmly against it before bringing them back together again. If you can do three tempos on the water without any mistakes, you will soon become a swimmer through daily practice.

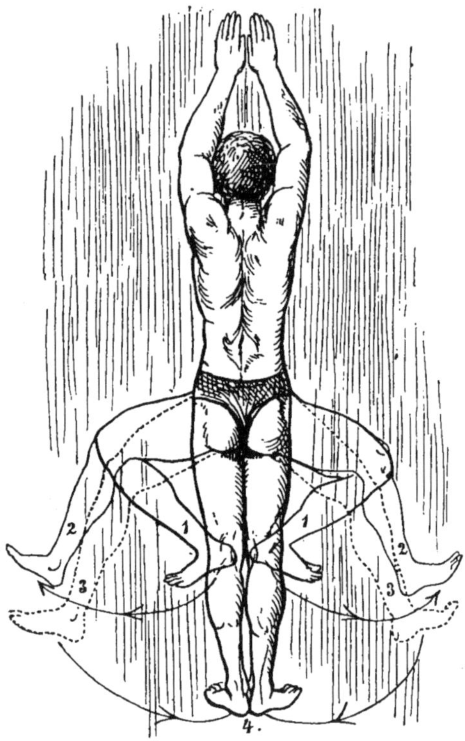

hero had little interest in picking up the grillparzer again, but she didn't want to leave it half-read. and so, in the evening, she went on to the fourth act.

ACT IV

Sestus: the Temple grounds. At the rear, the ocean. Toward the rear, left, Hero's tower: one window half faces the sea, the entrance is narrow with steps leading to it. Near by, on the beach, a clump of tall bushes; toward the front, left, the arches and columns of the adjacent houses. The right is an open view, with trees. A stone bench stands diagonally.

After the curtain rises, the voice of the Temp Guard is heard off-stage

TEMPLE GUARD This way, this way, you servants of the Temple!

she made it as far as the second scene.

Most swimmers are initially rather shy about diving; however, this fear is unfounded. Again, stand at the end of the diving board, facing the water, with your toes protruding, and use them to hold onto the edge. Then bend your upper body forward while simultaneously bending your knees slightly. At the same time, bring your hands forward so that your thumbs are against each other, your palms facing downward. At the moment you lose balance, your hands will come together in an outstretched position. The main thing is that you push yourself off the board with both feet at the last moment of falling into the water. The stronger the push, the further you will go.

ACT IV con't

Short stage. Right front, Leander's cottage. Beside it, a tree on which hangs a shrine with the image of a god.

NAUKLEROS *(enters and pauses before the cottage, stamps his foot on the ground)*
Leander, listen! Open the door, Leander!
So far, thanks to my care, he's right enough.
I left him here last evening safe inside;
And all this morning, so the neighbors say,
This door that's shut so tight has never opened.
But there's still no need to watch and guard, and worry.
Now why is he so slow? It's late enough.
Has his great grief — ? Or was his grief so great?
Perhaps, with pain and sorrow all forgotten,
He lies at ease, and dreams. Leander, ho!
You care-free sleepy-head! Now by the sun-god,
If you don't let me in, I'll break your door!
And yet, withal, it's strange; it's very strange —
(He peers through a crack in the door)
(Leander enters left rear)

LEANDER Ho there!

hero found leander's "ho there!" so crass that she angrily threw the book to the floor. as she did so, a folded piece of paper that she'd never noticed before slipped out. curious, she picked it up and read the first three stanzas of the following poem:

Two royal children once there were
Whose love would make you weep,
But they couldn't come together,
For the water was far too deep.

"Oh, dearest, can't you swim?
Then swim all the way out to me!
I want to light three candles,
And shine they should for thee."

But a deceitful nun heard it all
Pretending to be asleep;
She put out the candles one by one,
And the boy drowned there in the deep.

the almost seemingly fateful drift of chance, which provided her with such an appropriate theme relevant to her current situation, abruptly filled her with a great feeling of restlessness and soured her mood for the rest of the day. could the final line be an ominous prediction?

SATURDAY

Beware of jumping into the water or swimming underwater without first checking the depth. To practice staying below the water level for a long time, descend a staircase, holding onto the steps with both hands, until you reach the bottom.

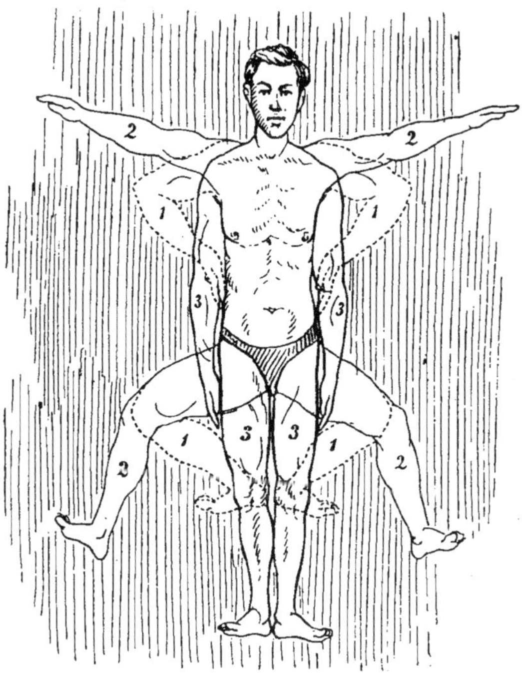

strangely enough, despite the previous day's confusion, hero had slept deep and long and woken up in an unexpectedly good mood. shooting up into sitting position, she noticed grillparzer's play on her bedside table. almost without thinking, she grabbed the book, opened the page with the bookmark and skimmed the beginning of the last act.

ACT V

Open place in front of Hero's tower as at the close of Act IV*. It is morning.*

When the curtain rises, Hero stands at the center of the stage, her head lowered and supported by her hand. Her eyes are fixed on the ground in front of her. Ianthe enters.

IANTHE What makes you stand so long and never move,
And stare at that one spot? Come to the wood.
The air has stilled its rage; the sea is calm.
But did you hear the tumult in the night?

HERO Indeed I heard.

IANTHE You stayed out here so late.

At last I did hear footsteps overhead:
And yet no light was showing from your room.

HERO No light! No light!

IANTHE There is some secret pains you

circa 5 p.m.

just as hero was sliding the 6th volume of grillparzer's edition back onto its old shelf in the library, she felt a light hand on her shoulder. it was that of the mother superior, praising her for reading his work. yes, the sea and all the rest! how does one achieve the exhilarating experience of unity-with-all-things??? the mother superior advised her to form six words that contained all the letters of the alphabet without repeating any of them. should she succeed in doing so satisfactorily, she would experience an overwhelming feeling of happiness . . .

hero pensively made her way to her cell.

as dusk began to fall and the room already lay in half-light, hero opened the cupboard in which she had stored various candles. nothing — the candles were either too thick or too thin, too short or too long. so she took the already lit candle from the window, blew it out, and pleasantly let the warm shaft glide through her fingers while a passage of romano guardini she'd recently read came to mind:

> Three times, in a rising tone, that is, with the highest solemnity, it was proclaimed:
> "This is the light." Three times the genuflection, that is, the act of adoration, responded. Thereafter the paschal candle was consecrated and lit on the flame which was brought in. The unspeakably beautiful hymn the Exsultet sung the candle's praises . . . Should piety only stand, as it were, before a closed iconostasis and venerate what lies behind it? Or is not everything based on what is called epiphany? . . . But it wants to bring back to consciousness a basic fact of our life which has been widely forgotten : namely, that this life takes place in the form of expression; of the execution of expression and the conception of expression . . .
> And yet man remains man. The organs are there; they must only be recognized, cared for and exercised. . . . But how does the eye once again become whole? The ear once again fully ear? The hand once again a human hand? From the object. . . . The organ and the object together form a whole, a relation, in which being takes place.

with the candle in one hand hero gently slid the other up and down its shaft, gently at first, gradually faster and faster. already in a state of excitement, she hurried to her bed, tossed the candle onto the linen, pulled the blanket over it then paused a few moments in silent fervor. after that she undressed and, feeling the increased moisture between her legs, slipped beneath the blanket. feeling the candle's hard roundness upon one thigh, she opened her legs and gently guided the candle between her spread labia. pressing it deeper — the now naked figure of the mother superior before her eyes — she began to move it with an increasing back and forth, all the while releasing ever more vigorous sounds of pleasure. then all of a sudden the bed, with her in it, rose from the floor and floated up into the air. in ecstasy, she yanked out the candle and with the singed wick scribbled the enigmatic words on the ceiling :

prumk zwoln gyxt,
vach qebs djif!

cake and prostheses

two dozen short prose texts

1

EARLY SHORT PROSE

(1949-56)

cake

his (thick) fingers fumble for the razorblade. yes, he says, yes, it's in the dictionary. in the morning her mouth tastes like toothpaste over and over. yes, those are his fingers, with their black-edged nails. and oily. back then, in the garage . . . he keeps on thinking. the glittering shards of glass. light: long across the naked mannequin. close enough to grab. parasol. utterly useless. mannequin. his fingers, the same ones which were fumbling for the raz . . . blade. in the dusky void of a display window (bombed-out shop). judge this activity. monday afternoon the . . . year-old . . . came upon a horrific death. sunrise: 3:57, sunset 7:51. "bring them back alive!" one dispenses with all formalities and hammers in one's nails. the ones outlined in black. his fingers clutch a soaked volume of the dictionary. first scare off the rats. rats — fingers . . . hardly any difference to the lecture. run over by the ambulance. the 49-year-old railway official h.s. was found yesterday at the intersection of . . . and every morning he grabs the shaving kit. please visit our advertising department, you will find a lot of new and beautiful things. asleep his fingers glide out from under the blanket, creep along the walls and all the protrusions that can be confused with a light switch, but aren't. only his nails become a bit lighter in the process (scraped brick lime), nude matte photos. on the basis of this unique opportunity you must not miss . . . yes, he says. every one of these movements is graceful. wire, papier-mâché and plaster. don't break it, you all! (yes.) even the flowers on the piano are cut by the falling glass pane. yes, and he smiles inexpressively. stares into the puddle. images images images — he walks the entire wharf pointing his submachine gun at the dark facades. later on his fingers (fingers!) rummage through the garbage clinging to the sewer grates. stubbornly. his fingers knead figures. something. out of bread. echoes from out of long dark halls . . . will be officially announced — — —. the hours trickle past. nails. dictionaries. mannequin stolen from a fashionable clothing store! use odol mouthwash. yes, he says. in the morning her mouth tastes like toothpaste. and every morning his fingers fumble for the razorblade, touch it, pick it up — he shaves. yes, he says. every morning. every morning.

a night in the waiting room

a leather jacket up by the high window of the waiting room, as if they belonged together. lord!

coffee, please. (though his sadness swam behind an upturned collar.)

it's cold.

(wrap yourself up good; maybe you can sleep.)

the guy in the leather jacket screamed: "no!"

at that disappointed and tired you sank into the cold smoke. your lips opening into damp clothing. bad air.

"good night!"

something made us increasingly unhappy. we looked around at a loss (you've got to look somewhere). dispersion! if only it were already late we'd dance. real wild.

across from the station the cheap hotels are waiting. up and down in front of them they move, one two, one two, like exhausted soldiers. the streets ran away from them, and they clung to the edges of a zero. the ground disappeared underfoot. handing over a cap to the porter for a modest tip.

i looked out the window. a fine rain moistened my face. thoughts in the solitude of a 2nd-class waiting room. night coming down. the city lights wake up. the hotels inch in.

the rhythm i give you is free. "so twitter across the parquet and take hold of my vibrating body. i will gladly be of help."

he sat upon her navel and gauged if it'd be enough. the wind made its way inside. the curtain swayed silently back and forth. –

no.

that's how i stepped out of line.

the backdrops fell over with a clap. millions of roses faded before the yellowed eyes of the organizers. truly a great moment! the entire dressing room burned out. once the smoke had cleared a bit, one could hear the muted chimes of a distant church clock . . .

midnight.

a shrouded face switched off the light.

hopped

the passengers laughed when the naked girl hopped from the hurtling train
twelve by the mail
the hospital had appeared to her in the glow of pale lights and twelve by the mail maybe already half past
she immediately fell into the bar the bar and twelve by the mail
and half-empty moldy baskets
and broken glasses
and you and i and
twelve by the mail
enough —
whether she drowned in the torrent of feverish ulcers of slow asters and oysters
stars
no one knows why
whether she thought she recognized him by higher command
who
twelve by the mail she fell out of bed broke her umbrella the rain streamed across her face hammered —
hammered — tumbling into the night like a shovel digging into the earth when it's burying time she was afraid
she heard the voice of the shaved pianos twelve by the mail twelve by the mail
she recognized the voice
and went silent
the passengers laughed but she remained silent
she got out of bed danced along the windowsill an entreaty and a hover
tumbling into the night like a shovel digging into the earth when it's burying time she didn't need to be afraid anymore

she heard a laugh her laugh and

silence

the door sprang wide open upon the switch the wind caressed her naked arms and she shivered shivered shivered her hair flew far far away to places people almost couldn't remember anymore — she looked out the wide-open door the night

the starlit night

she looked outside looked outside

sometimes in the office it was even nice just the train of hours after hour through the neighborhood his thundering penetrates the suburbs and all afternoon long hangs about the factory chimneys — drawn out — twelve by the mail twelve by the mail and over and over twelve by the mail twelve by the mail twelve by the mail after four weeks she had a collapse nothing more to be done to experience this play you don't even need 10 cents just twelve by the mail you've got to say twelve by the mail the siren is your last conquest

the company physician laid his ear to the typewriter to hear if it still beat — let us intone an ave maria for the health of the guests

the merry guests that was the decisive word she said understandable only with difficulty but keep on talking keep on talking don't ever stop don't ever stop keep on talking twelve by the mail twelve by the mail don't ever stop keep on talking keep on twelve by the mail twelve by the mail twelve by the mail

end of the tunnel

you know the moment when in a train right before coming out of a tunnel it gets brighter and brighter. a point of light constantly getting bigger until it takes up our whole field of vision. an old woman with an immense hump crouching down at the end of the tunnel. a pit in the light i am inexorably approaching. a pit in danger of collapse. suddenly i am there. i brush the hump with my arm. money? no. i can no longer pass. i have to toss my eyes into her furrows. i can't get them back, my eyes. down the shabby shirt. the creased leaves of her breasts. down, down. my kisses unexpectedly cover her startled hump. fat, dirt. my lips suck tight . . . i finally manage to tear them away. coin-sized holes punched into the flat breasts. spread across my naked knee. sieve. hey! just look at how i'm improving nature! no one there? no one there to admire my ornaments??? i want her to shit. a whole pile. spread the ornaments across her excrement. but she can't. all i can feel is the wetness of her anxiety-piss in my shoes. slice open her stomach to withdraw the scat myself? not yet. the temptation to lose my hands in rummaging about would be too great. you've got to rein in your passions, they say. but no, i am going to kill her. i am going to kill her so that there is an end to the temptations. i am going to tip the sunlight completely into the dark pit. redeem it. but where are the good intentions. my teeth bore through her withered lips — even though her whiskers prick. all the same my tongue breaks in. over the toothless gums. tumbling past holes and crests. deeper and deeper into the sources of her trickling spit. down, down
down
into the
abyss

on the phone

today french girls kept calling me on the phone — a strange day. one call after the other in more or less short intervals. without saying their names their voices penetrated my ear, and i had no idea what i was supposed to say. apart from a few words, i don't understand their language. which made their voices even more mysterious. toward evening the calls gradually began to ebb. but i remained sitting by the phone deep into the night.

desperate situation

the precautions i took have turned out to be entirely pointless the water relentlessly rushes in no one will be able to stop it my mother managed to leave the room just in time i myself hesitated to follow for just a few minutes but by then it was too late already it was probably meant to be my fate even if i can't come to terms with the thought of drowning the water is rising centimeter by centimeter and at an ever increasing rate now as far as i can tell it has already reached the chairs' seats damp spots are growing up the walls the soaked wallpaper is beginning to peel following my mother's departure in a fit of hopeless confusion i locked the door from inside and now feel incapable of unlocking it again now there can no longer be any talk of that and in the meanwhile without cease the level of the water has reached the handle in a moment i won't be able to open the window anymore my situation is hopelessly uplifting.

yes. or no?

going down the stairs of no where it wouldn't be possible for anyone to be the last going up the stairs of yes where it'd be impossible for everyone to be the first don't say whether you will say yes or no don't say where you are going because i know that you are always on your way to see me even though you don't recognize me whether you say yes or no is irrelevant (just as it is equally irrelevant whether you go up or down) if you recognize me you will no longer go if you don't you will always keep on going always on your way to me as if i were a plume of smoke not too close and not too far don't tell him that he's dead for then he could no longer die don't tell him that he's still alive don't show him any way out before he has made an effort to lay his hand between day and night

not enough yet

you haven't cried enough yet
he said   and pushed in her eyes
blood ran over her cheeks   he saw it   he was
confused   there was
no way to get her to cry anymore
and she hadn't cried enough yet
not by a long shot
and the blood confused him   there was no way to get her to cry anymore
you haven't cried enough yet
he bellowed   threw himself to the ground and buried his head in his hands   becoming aware of the fact that now he was lost   it would only be a matter of time
for she hadn't cried enough yet not by a long shot
her blood ran too soon
far too soon

sorrow

a thin strip of sorrow's hanging over the horizon the people who are leaving their houses are mechanically tearing off the buttons of their clothes while staring at the unusual event over and over in the meanwhile children are gathering the buttons off the ground to silently press them into piles of shit and enjoy the impressions they make others are tossing the buttons into the air to then look for them in vain and uncontrollably sob and wail over the irreparable loss

—

evenings when in the growing dusk lipstick and razorblades spin out of the tattered clouds a deep blue rush into the survivors' eyes the thin strip on the horizon has in the meanwhile inched significantly closer if no longer so clearly distinguishable

the sound

there was this sound i kept on following i didn't know why nor where it was leading me i pointlessly tried to ignore it but it was unignorably there every attempt to distract myself in vain every effort of my consciousness to remove me from the spell unsuccessful i kept on following the sound i had to follow the sound i pointlessly tried to get rid of it no argument was strong enough to change its direction or stop it neither asked nor said a thing sound just sound and i thought no and said yes and suddenly everything was filled by that yes i had unintentionally uttered and the sound came to me from all over the place enveloped me i had already crossed the border there was no going back and the intensity of the sound continued to grow i felt my body assume its vibrations i became wonderfully heavy and let myself fall it didn't hurt on the contrary felt indescribably good i found myself right in the middle of the sound and was perfectly happy at one with the sound beyond yes and no

a manuscript of napoleon

it'd be best for me to begin with a line in napoleon's hand

"the battle will . . ."

that's what it says there the rest illegible the strokes seem to have been blurred by some kind of corrosive liquid and what comes next is probably of little interest it's got to do with the opening a good opening says just about everything still here i must conclude prematurely conclude someone will perhaps complain a sudden migraine prevents me from continuing to spin this all too happily found thread

fragmentary memories

involuntarily he locked . . . such a young man . . . his . . . would you look at that, my name in the paper . . . first emergency room . . . oh horror . . . shameful . . . pushed it aside . . . the doctor . . . yes, that's right — the doctor from back then . . . diphtheria . . . he rushed to the children's hospital . . . only dared with words . . . the pupils of a corpse . . . the skull should . . . my . . . will anyone sleep . . . try to rest . . . with this i give . . . i . . . it will . . . me . . .

agony the gaze . . . to come back even when for him the first . . . see . . . heard excitedly . . . otherwise unafraid . . . premature . . . hysteria . . . my hands . . . innocent . . . on my account . . . the wave . . . during the day . . . punctually performed an embarrassing examination . . .

weakness . . .

unquiet . . . his promise . . . it was even in . . . frightened to death . . . in front of my eyes . . . i will be . . . want to sleep . . .

the following are dreams . . . furiously arouses . . . screams . . . peace through the mental relief of the fork . . . he presented it in vain to the stranger the following day . . . distant . . . where there is no disturbance . . . the morning brings . . . therefore . . .

recovered? . . .

the hat wasn't shot by a guard . . . listen . . . immediately he . . . a visitor: . . . thank god it's you . . . we're amazed . . .

2

RECENT SHORT PROSE

(2018)

some events on the morning of february 19

to start with something slid out of her hands as she hastily turned the corner. then a car drove into another. covered in blood its driver yelled: "one in the afternoon!" the indicated time matched that on the watch of a dapper young man — if not one hour later for by then he was already in new york. a reason to disregard him as a witness. in the meanwhile numerous apartments had burst into flame, and just a little while later an entire façade. there! an ear-splitting crash!!! in a nearby district a busy bridge collapsed, crushing a swallow which had just stopped to rest on the railing. the woman, from whose hand something had slid, looked through her tote bag for the missing piece. after a futile search she took a few steps closer and spoke to the driver of the heavily damaged front car. they exchanged a few words. then she disappeared. upon awaking he suddenly remembered her name: emmi sumek.

trains of thought

going somewhere is more enjoyable than coming from somewhere. sometimes, of course, when going there somehow you are coming from somewhere, which is just as true the other way around. in any event the excitement of going forth far exceeds that of going somewhere, especially when the going is upwards. less enjoyable is an aimless going back and forth, even if it often approaches going, but on the other hand makes going home increasingly difficult. going home and going about are closely related, though mostly far apart. by the way, there are some who go out without ever taking a single step — no wonder, as going out and proceeding are mutually exclusive. at any rate always or all the same. unless you go back, for example, whence you originally came or to where you ended up. in any event, it should not be forgotten that keeping going forth apart from going away can, under certain circumstances, make you insecure and lead to mere walking.
what's best is to fundamentally avoid anything unnecessary.

drape and curtain

the window is open. the wind prances in and nestles the trembling drape to its neighboring curtain, which — awoken — with a painfully upright posture tries to change position. it's only a partial success — but where is there to go?
herr gudrun steps in, leaving the door ajar. there's a big draft. a gust of wind tears the curtain off its runner and blows it through the window right out onto the street. there it helplessly staggers back and forth before slipping beneath a passing car. soiled, it is now stretched out with no idea what to do. already the next car is crushing the barely recognizable curtain. can you even call it that? over the next few days, these first cars will be followed by an infinite number of others. and — not to forget! — shoes. countless numbers of shoes, as is their wont, thoughtlessly trampling the severely injured curtain.
poor shreds!

a casual consideration of money

there are two different types of money: paper money and coin. the former is as flat as an elevator stuck on the tenth floor, which demands an unreasonable amount of patience from its occupants. indeed making people wait is one of the specific behavioral modes of money, which typically takes a steep dive starting at a hundred — and at a clip, too, which has already led to countless fatal accidents and will undoubtedly continue to do so. as far as paper money is concerned, self-professing catholics may enjoy the pleasant fact that they can eat it without any second thoughts if on a pilgrimage to mariazell, but only if they truly believe in claims like the "immaculate conception." if, however, they happen not to take such things literally but only figuratively, that is, if their belief is essentially just a kind of sham, then their meal of paper money will be utterly indigestible and will lead to seemingly endless bloating, sometimes even for years. such relativization is the only unforgivable sin. a lucky penny found by chance can be mistaken for a wink from above, that is, a kind of annunciation without ramifications, but it cannot in any way compete with the immaculate conception itself. the word "luck" is therefore without any value.
there are widely differing opinions on the question of whether money has more to do with numerals or numbers. since the introduction of the monetary system, the dispute has repeatedly led to bitter battles, such as the thirty years' war and the devastating world wars of the past century. in the end the only victor has been inflationary counterfeit money, the cause of severe earthquakes and gigantic floods.
in order to keep money handy, purses with not entirely harmless locks were put into circulation early on. they are often much more expensive than their contents and are therefore used as alternative containers for smaller quantities of fallen fruit. compared to coin, paper money has the annoying disadvantage of not being able to rest quietly on the tabletop, but being in rather constant and violent motion, whereby a mere

draft is also the frequent cause of such annoying agitation. coin, on the other hand, cannot be crumpled nor torn to shreds, just rolled into the gutter with hardly a dent at all. which is why it is excellent for tender caresses, especially between eight and nine o'clock in the evening. paper money, on the other hand, allows you to snort unhindered and, thanks to it, satisfy a number of other needs. and thus the frequently heard expression "money doesn't stink" is incorrect. odorless money shortages, on the other hand, are like a helicopter that always lands in the wrong places, causing swallowing inhibitions that are prohibitively expensive to cure. it is therefore advisable to bridge long waiting times in bad company with an espresso lungo and a game of marked cards.

the collection bag

a collection bag is dangling through the rows of pews. what would the church and its billions be without the small donations of the poorest of the poor! after the rows on the left, it is now the turn of those on the right. it already sounds a bit fuller. the church can use every cent, regardless of what it's for. that's what makes collection so much fun. though the daily grind is hardly worth it, sundays, when a number of naifs unexpectedly find themselves in the house of the tripartite god, see quite a lot come together. god's servant is pleased with small contributions too, no matter who they come from. when the sums are large and larger the noble donor is even worth a prayer of thanks from god's servants. love thy neighbor as thyself. for the more intimately you love yourself, the more you love the noble donor. that is quite clear. how beautiful and uplifting it is to stroll through the rows swinging the collection bag with a look of devotion on one's face. how meaningful the life of god's servants, these sly shepherds of a mostly negligible number of lambs. may it last a long time still and may the arm with the collection bag never flag. for ever and ever amen.

holidays

in german, when holidays show up one at a time, they are considered feminine, in the second case, the genitive, they become masculine, which changes nothing about the fact that they are essentially pointless. where do they come from, do they have an acceptable background, a trustworthy lineage? the answer is a clear and resounding "no." but over the course of time they have obtained a few cheap attributes. for example their egg-like form. originally they were probably known as eggdays, for, like sundays, a day of rest, those are the days you eat an egg for breakfast — either a soft-boiled egg, that is, one boiled for a little less time, or a hard-boiled egg, which is also enjoyable cold. no less beloved is the classic fried egg with bacon, this time around warm once again. and so you can tuck into the holiday with a fork, or spoon it out of an appropriately shaped cup.

in theory every holiday ends at midnight, yet in practice they last until the moment you fall asleep, which is sometimes late in the day. holidays are unreliable journeymen and can hardly agree on certified dates. they do, however, generally prefer the beginnings of the week or saturdays, so as to ingratiate themselves with sundays and together extend the day's dread a little longer still. this can lead to disturbing cracks within your four walls.

the seasons have a strange influence on holidays' appearance and character. in spring, they have split hooves of hard-dried strudel dough and during the day prowl the horse stables, intoxicating themselves with their spicy scent — something that makes them unusually peaceful in the evening. in summer they stretch out and love to lounge on overcrowded beaches on deckchairs, their songs so soft that even with a hearing tube you only catch the faintest whisper. in the fall holidays like to be jovial and, when the weather is poor, leaf for hours through fashion magazines from times gone by. in winter they often get out of control. sometimes you might even catch them going to church, which is extremely embarrassing for them the following day if asked about it. there have, however, already been holidays that were shooed away after a short existence to make room for newly appointed ones. in any event, we should critically examine the justification of long-established holidays, even if the prospect of success remains rather slim under current circumstances.

the prosthesis

don't forget your prosthesis!
doesn't matter, it's right there, next to you, even if, at the moment, you haven't got it wedged between your rotting canines. still a little preserved for you as a language-garbler right there in that cave of yours. think a bit before you start to blabber and run out of steam. like a mother the prosthesis hangs thoughtfully between the rest of your halfway usable canines. like a mother that feeds you, that wants the best. you've just had a spot of luck, you've won as well as lost, you hole-ridden-pair-of-house-slippers-in-need-of-tender-loving-care, you. have you already considered the fact that you're a prosthesis yourself? a prosthesis just a tad more rickety than the one in your mouth already. yeah, just mess about a bit, spit the single sounds out in a row so that, even if they're tough to hear, one can read them clearly enough:

> the prosthesis is a brazen liar,
> the prosthesis is a devious fop,
> the prosthesis is a very fragile thing.

you non-thing you.
you long-since-convicted liar you.
you exhausted fop!

the terrible thirst. a crime story

eva, doris, yvonne, berta, zita, norbert, quirin, alfred, paul, friedrich, oswald, xenia, waltraud, helga, vera, tobias, klaus, martha, ursula, georg, robert, josef, ludwig, irene, susanne, christian — and those are just the ones who managed to drag themselves here on their last legs. tormented by a terrible thirst. what's to be done? far and wide not a thing to drink. city reservoir dry to the last drop. all the bars closed. already low on water beforehand instead of bread, rolls, croissants, or pretzel sticks the bakeries have nothing but meter-high mounds of quicksand. where did it come from? who knows? folks say they should've kept their windows and doors closed. on the asphalt of the dust-covered streets the first six hundred-and-seventy-nine people dying of thirst are rolling about, wheezing and groaning for god's mercy. water, water, beer or wine — the calls fade as soon as they're heard, to no avail. in vienna general hospital a guy gets himself together and smites his already comatose neighbor with an empty jug. now one at least has been released. but what about the countless others? what, what???!!!

affection

when tender affection's fine threads softly move, touch, snuggle, and connect, the wardrobes, tables, chairs breathe, beds a barely audible in and out, inch closer together, closer and closer, until the room
    becomes a crowded bird's nest,
    where not a single resident can forget having soared over town.

tears

what all happens with tears. we wipe them away as if simply water, but there's a whole bunch of chemicals inside: leucine-enkephalin, lysozyme and prolactin. the first is said to be similar to morphine in its effects — if that wasn't enough to make you cry! and what deep satisfaction when they, tears, roll silently down, you could funnel them into an empty matchbox and keep them dried up there in your desk. tears! where do they come from, where do they run? questions upon questions! did you know that, every day in germany alone, an estimated 40 bathtubs of tears are produced? most often between 6 and 11 p.m. as a man who only cries around 17 times a year i already sense that women cry up to 64 times. crying, with or without a reason, is supposed to be healthy. just to make myself happy, i would like to have a big old tear set in a ring — modern science will manage — to wear on the fourth finger of my right hand. if only to remember.

like butter

in the austrian dictionary, "butter" appears between "büttel" ("bailiff") — the messenger of the court, who still comes right below "büste" (you got it, "busts") — and "butzen," that is, the core, say, of apples and pears, e.g., or "butzenscheibe" (crown-glass windows) and "bzw." (an abbreviated form of "or rather"), the latter the last entry among the b's. in the german duden dictionary "butter" appears between "büttenpapier" (handmade paper) and "butterfly," which might remind you of puccini's opera of the same name — butter is by nature silent, which no doubt contributes to its high degree of popularity, at least among those who, as we say, "have butter on their heads" (which is to say, a guilty conscience) instead of a hat. normally, as far as butters go, buttered bread and buttered rolls are engaged in a constant feud, each considering itself the better. and yet, as there is not the slightest sound, such disagreements remain unnoticed. which is why butter is considered a rather peaceful being. nevertheless, if you smear something other than butter on someone's butter sandwich, which would be even more difficult in the case of a butter roll, displeasure ensues. be that as it may, this state of affairs annoys butter sandwiches to no end. at short notice, butter itself, both systematically and in terms of length, might come up short, but, in principle, it is available on weekdays from five in the morning until 4 a.m. the following morning. on sundays and holidays, in case of emergency, butter must be woken up immediately, whereupon it usually takes on highly disconcerting forms. but don't be fooled : forms are transient, even if often confusing.

butter comes in both soft and hard states. in large quantities, soft butter is suited for romantic boat trips, while in a hard state conveniently packed for summertime snowball fights.

the forgetting, an object

the forgetting, a hard object of uncertain shape cocooned in strips of tape, growing up and over me and suddenly there in the form of a gothic cathedral — burned down to the ground in the last war, so far — right in the middle of the room, swaying on a wide, bare stretch of ground, and hungry. for more and more. for a plate of pasta, for raspberries, for ice-cubes, for hammers and sickles, for space shuttles and many an unknown thing. with an oppressive smell of galactic dust. of asphyxiated fish in the wardrobe, of house slippers of various size and a scruffy, un-ironed suit. the object bows and briefly coughs the remains of the cathedral off the table — now the space is empty. my head covering clatters like a typewriter that someone's just begun to use. masses of hailstones fill the carriage of a train derailing at full speed. when all of a sudden broken windowpanes offer a glimpse into night's deep dark. the heavy clots on my hands and face must be blood. in the middle of the room there's a cedar tree, draped with apples. i take an axe and knock holes in the parquet, succeeding in nothing but making holes. here and there a few illuminated gothic letters appear : evoking the names, the images of friends and acquaintances of mine who've already died, before, shortly thereafter, disappearing once more.

GERHARD RÜHM was born in Vienna, Austria, in 1930. A writer, composer, and visual artist, he is truly one of the key figures of the postwar European avant-garde. With his earliest work dating to the late 1940s, he was one of the first practitioners of concrete poetry and a founding member of the legendary Wiener Gruppe in the 1950s. His lifelong study of music has had a lasting impact on his multifaceted work with its amalgams of music and language and image and text. The result has been a decades-long exploration of a broad range of forms — poetry, prose, radio plays, drama scenarios, musical compositions, visual compositions, collages, and graphic art — drawing on a lineage that can be traced to Dadaism, Surrealism, and Dark Romanticism. His more recent work cleverly incorporates pornographic motifs while skewering the Church and regularly invoking the aesthetics of ugliness, vulgarity, and banality. Rühm has received numerous awards, including the Austrian State Prize in 1991 and the America Award in Literature in 2022. He currently divides his time between Cologne and Vienna.

ALEXANDER BOOTH, originally from Virginia, is a poet, translator, and printmaker who has lived in Berlin for the past decade after having spent many years in Rome. The recipient of support from the German Translators' Fund and PEN America, his translations from German include work by Friederike Mayröcker, Alexander Kluge, Jürgen Becker, Lutz Seiler, and a new translation of Ludwig Wittgenstein's *Tractatus Logico-Philosophicus*.

GERHARD RÜHM

cake & prostheses

mini dramas and short prose

translated by Alexander Booth from the original German:

drei personen wollen guter laune sein. minidramen
(Klagenfurt und Graz: Ritter Verlag, 2017)

hero liest grillparzer / leander lernt schwimmen. eine klassische liebes-geschichte | *kuchen und prothesen. zwei dutzend kurzprosatexte*
(Klagenfurt und Graz: Ritter Verlag, 2019)

cover: "sound figure," manuscript paper collage, 2005
frontispiece: melogram, pencil on manuscript paper, 1987
flyleaf: silhouette from the series Organic and Geometric Forms, 1999

Grillparzer extracts from *Hero and Leander: Tragedy in Five Acts*,
trans. by Henry Harmon Stevens (Yarmouth Port: Register Press, 1938)

Layout and design by Silk Mountain

Set in Futura PT

FIRST EDITION

Published in 2024 by
Twisted Spoon Press
P.O. Box 21 — Preslova 12
150 00 Prague 5
Czech Republic
www.twistedspoon.com

Printed and bound in the Czech Republic
by TISKÁRNA PROTISK, České Budějovice

TRADE DISTRIBUTION:

UK / Commonwealth / Europe
CENTRAL BOOKS
www.centralbooks.com

US / Canada
SCB DISTRIBUTORS
www.scbdistributors.com